"*Circle of Peace* breathes new life into these ancient Greek myths for a new generation of readers to enjoy."

—G.G. KELLNER, author of *Hope, A History of the Future*

"Sophia Kouidou-Giles is a master storyteller who can make faraway places and long-ago times feel like they are here and now."

—THEO NESTOR, author of *Writing is My Drink*

"A captivating retelling of a Greek myth. Sophia Kouidou-Giles delights us from beginning to end in this modern retelling of the sorceress Circe. Inventive and captivating, *An Unexpected Ally* deserves a sequel."

—SUSAN AYRES, professor and poetess,
author of *Walk Like the Bird Flies*

"*Circle of Peace* is very highly recommended reading for readers who enjoy twists on traditional stories of the Greek gods . . . [it's] fiction that sizzles with an action, insight, and a reimagined mythology worthy of discussion and debate."

—MIDWESTERN REVIEW

"While the house of Helios works to turn tragedy into a movement for peace, others prefer to sow the seeds of war and unrest, leading to a battle of wills of mythic proportions. *Circle of Peace* is an imaginative tale you won't soon forget."

—Maria A. Karamitsos, author, poet, & former publisher, and founder of Windy City Greek magazine

"Sophia Kouidou-Giles captures the nuances of Greek legend with elegance, clarity, and wit. . . . This book explores loss, resilience, and the enduring quest for peace despite all odds. I highly recommend *Circle of Peace* to anyone who loves mythology, particularly Greek myths and legends!"

— Readers' Favorite, FIVE STARS

CIRCLE OF
PEACE

CIRCLE OF PEACE

A GREEK TALE OF PERSE'S GREAT HALL

SOPHIA KOUIDOU-GILES

SHE WRITES PRESS

Published 2025

Printed in the United States of America

Print ISBN: 978-1-64742-848-8
E-ISBN: 978-1-64742-849-5
Library of Congress Control Number: 2024918850

For information, address:
She Writes Press
1569 Solano Ave #546
Berkeley, CA 94707

Interior design and typeset by Katherine Lloyd, The DESK

She Writes Press is a division of SparkPoint Studio, LLC.

"Only those who will risk going too far
can possibly find out how far one can go."
—T. S. Eliot

CONTENTS

PART I

PART II

PART I

Muses of Pieria who give glory through song, come hither, tell of Zeus your father and chant his praise. Through him mortal men are famed or unfamed, sung or unsung alike, as great Zeus wills. For easily he makes strong, and easily he brings the strong man low; easily he humbles the proud and raises the obscure, and easily he straightens the crooked and blasts the proud,—Zeus who thunders aloft and has his dwelling most high.

—Hesiod, *Works and Days*, 1–10
(trans. Hugh Gerard Evelyn-White)

ONE

ARRIVAL

*I*n a dusty chiton, Queen Perse wended up the path to her palatial home, the two-story marble fortress of one thousand rooms. Porters lugged packages behind her, up the terraced hill from the harbor. Her husband, Helios, was not there to welcome her—the sun-god was busy riding his chariot on the daily trek, from east to west, delivering the life-force of sunlight over the earth.

The queen's arrival had set off a commotion. House servants ran to the columned entrance, picked up her parcels, and carried them to her wing. An eager young man reached out to relieve her of the hefty satchel she held.

"No. Not this one," Perse scolded.

"My queen," he answered obediently, opening a parasol and raising it to protect her from the scorching sun. He walked slightly behind her.

Tall and energetic, the queen moved quickly down the corridor and up the steps to the second floor that led to her quarters. Frescoes depicting Oceanid nereids dancing, swimming, and playing with Perse's young son, Aeetes, and her daughter, Circe, decorated the walls. Reaching her bedroom, she set down the satchel containing the magnificent prize from the blacksmiths of Athens.

Alerted by a runner, her chambermaid, Leonora, was already preparing the queen's bath. The young woman worked hurriedly, carrying hot water to the small, round pool next to the bedroom, a pool decorated with mosaics of bright orange sea anemones stretching their tentacles to catch passing fish, and a pair of playful dolphins entwined on the floor.

"Greetings. What aromatics have you added, Leonora?" Perse asked, shedding her clothes and removing her sandals. She stepped into the warm water.

Leonora handed her two jars. "Would you like rose or ivy salts, my mistress?"

Perse poured some rose salts into the water and sat on the pool steps to soak, ready to listen to Leonora's welcome and to the palace news.

"We have missed you, my queen. The sun-god has been tracking you, telling us you will come home soon. You have been away a lot."

"He does not make it easy to be with him," Perse said with a sigh. She plunged into deeper water. Then, watching her maid bring out some oils she liked to use after her bath, the queen remained silent, waiting for Leonora's report.

"He has been favoring Clymene in your absence," said the maid.

"So, my sister, his old flame, is center stage again," answered Perse, wondering if her husband deserved her return.

"Helios is proud of their son, Phaethon, and spoils both him and his mother. But you are the queen. She is just one of his many consorts. Do you remember when her boy turned thirteen years old? They had recently settled in the palace. We celebrated his birthday in the Great Hall, and Helios was present himself. You would have thought the child was an Olympian god. The boy is becoming impossible. Constant demands and tantrums. His mother has her hands full with him," said Leonora.

"Here, massage my back and neck," Perse ordered her maid. "It's not like my husband to spoil anyone but himself. He asked me to come back. I just happen to be the one he favors today. Do you know what he wants from me?"

Perse stepped out of the pool and wrapped herself in a thick towel. She knew well that although she was free to travel and visit other places, her husband expected her to serve and remain faithful to him. However, in Helios's palace, bedding more than one partner was acceptable for men, just as it has always been for Zeus and other Olympian gods.

"I doubt he called you back for Phaethon's fifteenth birthday celebration alone," remarked her maid. "Is he working on forging a new alliance? By the way, the boy's birthday celebration is in a few days." Leonora finished massaging her shoulders and sprayed her favorite perfume on Perse's wrists, behind her ears, and on her chest. The immortal queen, youthful and refreshed, asked for a mirror and golden glitter to dust on her eyelids. She wanted to look her best for him.

Helios had summoned his wife with a note delivered to her by a carrier pigeon at their daughter Circe's palace. His message was brief: *Come home. You will not regret it.* Was he finally going to build her the new palace wing with a Great Hall, as she had been demanding? She had welcomed the thought of returning home because she was tired of roaming the Mediterranean and missed the palace life. It was also time to mend her relationship with Helios; it had been sagging in recent months. Her ambition superseded her love for him and created friction between them. Tired of his demands, she aimed for independence and hoped the days he presumed to order her around would soon be over.

In the past, Helios and Perse had created powerful alliances with the Olympians. They had a reputation for being an excellent team. They had even gained Zeus's favor, especially after Helios recognized him as the father of all gods. Zeus had returned the gesture by calling Helios, the son of Titan Hyperion, god above all others, and Hyperion himself.

Facing the garden, refreshed and dry, the queen sat on a bench and held a mirror to watch as Leonora styled her blonde hair, drawing it into an elaborate bun, letting curls drop onto her forehead. Perse asked for her pair of sunburst earrings, Helios's gift, and added several rows of golden chains around her neck. Leonora applied the glitter to her eyelids. A younger servant brought in a silk lilac peplos and artfully draped the long shawl in loose folds over Perse's shoulder. Court etiquette called for the sun-god's wife to enter the throne room well-groomed and in grand style.

An hour later, the queen walked into the Great Hall, followed by two courtesans. She carried her satchel. A pair of trumpeters stationed by the entrance raised their bronze salpinges, long trumpetlike instruments, to announce her. All whispering stopped when she arrived. She looked around the sunny hall, smiling at those who bowed, and rested her eyes on the magic tapestry her daughter, enchantress Circe, had woven for her father. Helios had prominently displayed it behind his throne. It was a lavish arras, painting a field of spring flowers, their blossoms and leaves swaying in constant motion, caressed by the sun and invisible breezes. It was breathtaking. Pride and envy gripped Perse for her talented daughter. It was a prickly feeling because mother and daughter had fallen apart, yet Circe still had a closer relationship with her father. Their daughter ruled over Aeaea, an island in the Aegean Sea, and their son, Aetees, ran his kingdom of Colchis, near the east end of the Black Sea. Although distances did not have to keep them apart, their busy lives made visits between them rare.

The queen always felt the weight of her strained relation-ship with her daughter. Although she kept it to herself, she felt a sense of disappointment and frustration toward Circe, whom she considered stubborn and resistant to conforming to her sta-tus as a goddess. Perse had cultivated an image of success, and sought admiration and respect, a trait the queen sensed that Circe considered as shallow. Deep down, Perse yearned for a chance to reconcile and rebuild her bond with Circe.

The small crowd in the grand hall included as usual junior members of the guard in light armor, several couples, lady friends from town, and guests of the palace from land and sea. In the far corner, her sister, the nereid Clymene, was paying rapt attention to Orion, a handsome young man her son knew, when Perse's noisy entrance disrupted their chat. Hearing the commotion, she peered sideways, and when she saw who it was, she dropped the conversation, picked up her long tunic, and rushed to greet her sister with a hug.

"You came! I hoped you would." As she laughed with delight, Clymene's plump cheeks and sharp chin quivered with excitement. "I love your perfume! Lovely fragrance. How was your trip, sister?"

"Tired of roaming. Glad to be home. Where is Helios?" said Perse, her eyes checking the hall for dignitaries. A pair of nere-ids waved to her, as did a couple of minor gods, but the rest were mostly commoners.

"Here. Let me lighten your load. Is it a gift?" Clymene smiled delightedly.

Perse nodded. "A surprise."

Clymene offered, "Helios will be back tonight."

Perse would not let go of the satchel. In it she carried her special gift for Helios, a set of bridles buckled with gold for his fire-darting horses. She had expected that he would wait to receive her at the Great Hall. He was late tonight. She meant the gift as her peacemaking gesture, a truce, to bring an end to their recent battles. Perse had abandoned the palace for a few weeks to "visit family and friends" after another epic argument with her husband about her demand to have her own Great Hall. All he did was laugh, dismissing her. She still remembered his last words: "One Great Hall is enough." *We shall see*, she thought. Because even walls offer no privacy in a palace, the chief gossips suspected that the true cause of Perse's departure was the argument. It was not the first time.

Hooking her arm with her sister's, Perse moved to a shady bench in the garden with a view of the verdant hillsides, alive with the color of spring poppies. She hoped for a quiet conversation with Clymene. "Where is he?" the queen asked her sister, fanning herself, for it was a warm summer day. "What is his mood this week?"

"He is spending more time with his sister, Selene, goddess of the moon." Clymene's eyes softened. "He wants you to be here for Phaethon's birthday celebration. My son is turning fifteen!"

"Where is my nephew?"

"You won't recognize him! Your nephew is a young man, smart and strong. He is away on a hunt with his friends." Clymene's voice pulsed with pride. "They return tomorrow."

"I noticed Phaethon portrayed in the new fresco along the corridor of the Great Hall. The one that shows Helios riding his chariot to bring the morning light on earth. Phaethon is watching him, smiling his radiant smile. Beautiful!" Perse stroked her necklace and, leaning closer to Clymene, spoke in confidential tones: "Who is Helios courting these days?" They shared that pain.

Clymene narrowed her eyes. "Not sure. I don't need to know. He will tell you if you ask."

There was nothing more to gain from this conversation, so Perse returned to the main hall and her sister followed. A younger couple approached the queen to ask about her trip and hear news she had picked up during her travels. Perse chatted with them aimlessly for a while and then focused on the end of the ten-year war in Troy and its aftermath. It was still the major topic of conversation at many royal courts. The news she shared was good for the Greeks, thanks to crafty Odysseus, the king of Ithaca; many admired his plan. "Circe told me that under his command, the Greek warriors built a wooden horse and hid in its belly. The Trojans believed the Greeks were gone, opened the gates to the city, and brought the horse inside. That night, the Greeks crept out and sacked Troy, massacred its men, and carried off its women. It was the will of Zeus," Perse said.

But the couple of courtesans did not agree. "There are a few of us who had relatives in Troy. I have been weeping. With no news, we hope our people have survived. I hate the savagery of the Greeks," the woman lamented.

Clymene interjected graciously, "I am sad for your people's bad fortune." She was familiar with the latest news and, bored with their chatter, excused herself to return to her conversation with the same eager young man.

Later that night, Perse awoke from a deep sleep with Helios's gentle kiss on her forehead. She opened her eyes and blinked in his light. Although startled, she smiled, stretched like a cat, and rubbed her eyes and temples.

"We have missed you, dear. Good to have you back home," he whispered. "How are Circe and Aeetes?"

"All is well," Perse answered in a groggy voice, sitting up. She watched his eyes resting on the curves of her bare bosoms and covered herself with the sheet. She watched him crawl next to her like he used to in the good old days. Only the soothing burble of the garden waterfall interrupted the quiet of the night. Perse kept her distance, moving a smidgen away.

She debated whether to hold his hand, maybe even embrace him. She had missed him, but they had not seen each other in a month and some things needed sorting out before she would allow more intimacies. "We are celebrating Phaethon's birthday the day after tomorrow," she said, "and I need to get him a gift. Have you thought about what you would give him?"

Helios shifted closer to her. "His mother told him I am his father. He is excited, still taking that in. I will come up with something . . . something to prove to him I love and value my son."

"You have always been a generous father," she answered, reaching for her fan. "I came unprepared for his celebration; I was responding to your bidding. How are you?"

She heard him sigh, and then he spoke his sister's name. "The moon, Selene." She knew how close they were. When he was upset about her affairs, it was difficult to soothe him. He always answered Selene's cries for help.

Helios poured out his worries. She listened to him and watched his eyes dart around the room. She knew he was making certain there were no curious ears around. On family matters, they were both careful about gossip and rumors. "It's about Selene," he repeated. "She is bedding down a mortal shepherd, and Zeus disapproves. He is a demanding man. Why fall for such a character? What is the matter with my sister? I begged her to find someone else, but she is deeply in love. Zeus is ready to punish them both. I asked him to give me a chance to intercede before it is too late."

Perse feared Zeus's wrath. Her imagination flared up. No one could tell what punishment might await the couple. The god of thunder and lightning could strike and burn both lovers, but then the twenty-four hours would be split between Helios and his second sister, Eos, the goddess of dawn. It would be a true burden for them all if Selene was gone.

The queen got out of bed and moved to the window, staring at the pale quarter moon. She spoke slowly. "Passion is a dangerous thing. I feel for your sister, but I agree with Zeus. Who is this manipulative and ambitious human? Is he pressing Selene?"

Helios sighed again. He sat up in bed, and she saw his facial muscles tighten. "His name is Endymion. Selene has borne him fifty daughters! She confessed to me that she visits him every night—when the moon comes down from the sky. She loves him so much she can't bear the thought of his death."

"How can I be of help to you, my husband?" Perse asked, and turned away to hide a smile. He needed her.

"I know you can come up with ways to avoid disaster. Invite to Phaethon's birthday anyone you can influence to help us out, my dear," he said, looking glum. She could hardly hear him mumble to himself: "Will she give him up? I will press her to."

"I think Hestia, the goddess of hearth and home, is an excellent candidate, or perhaps Athena, but they will not come to this celebration. They have access to Zeus, but would they support a mortal? They might visit us, taste our hospitality someday . . . if only we had proper quarters to offer them . . . But it would be best to go to them in person."

"Do invite them, by all means."

"You see them every day! You want my help, but you do not value me enough."

"Why do you say that?" Helios was on his feet, moving toward a door hidden by a heavy tapestry that led to his quarters.

Perse returned to her bed. "It would be much easier to impress my guests and get Hestia's help if I had my hall, husband. It would serve us both."

"We *have* a hall, a pretty fine hall." He sounded annoyed. That troubled Perse because she knew his refusal was not about the effort and cost. He was standing in her way. The queen wanted to create her own allies, like Athena and Hera, and perhaps even Cybele, the revered mother of all gods and humans, if she could get a suitable setting to invite them to. She had to have her own Great Hall to be worthy of such visitors. It was really no surprise to Perse that Cybele had never responded to her past invitations.

Her dream was that together with Cybele and other Olympian goddesses, she would start an alliance of women seeking a better balance in a world ruled by the hegemony of Zeus.

Helios lifted the tapestry, and before he vanished, he finished with a tired plea. "Let's think about more ways tomorrow morning. The time is short, but you are clever, Perse."

Perse rose from her bed and looked at him. "Your hall is good enough for Phaethon's celebration, but not for the Olympian gods." There was defiance in her voice. "I will see if I can be of help."

TWO

PERSE
AT THE STABLES

*A*ctivity started before dawn at Helios's stables, hours before the sun would leave his palace to sprinkle daylight on the earth. Busy young men from Egypt, dark and muscly, fed and groomed noble Aethon, Eous, Phlegon, and Pyrois, his well-trained horses. Bred for speed and endurance, perfect companions for the charioteer, they knew his every wish, followed his every command, traveling the heavenly heights and shifting orbits to adjust for the seasons. The foursome lived in adjoining paddocks, tended by men trained in Egypt, whisperers, talented stable hands. This morning, they had been fed and were snorting and swishing their tails, expecting Helios's impending arrival.

The queen had emerged from her rooms before daybreak, wearing a light tiara and a simple purple tunic, energetic and bubbly. She planned to meet her husband at the stables before his daily trek. Her eyes were dancing with mischief as she picked up the satchel. "He doesn't know," she told Leonora, who had admired the bridles at her mistress's urging. "Do you think he will like my gift?"

"It's perfect. He will love it," her maid said, helping Perse

13

don her chiton, an overcoat to ward off the early morning chill.

An attendant followed her down the corridors and out of the palace, ready to meet her every wish. Perse had him carry the satchel to the stables and, once they got there, ordered him to take the contents out and hang all four fine sets of bridles on the arena fence.

Before long, the grooms who had finished feeding and brushing the horses and tidying the paddock were crowding around her to see what she had brought. The queen knew they admired the bridles, even though they spoke to each other in a foreign language. Perse watched them pick them up, check the strength of the leather, touch the gilded buckles, and try the adjustments. They seemed eager to fit them on the horses. Another pair of expert grooms arrived, their skin mellow brown, curious about the growing excitement. The queen watched their dark brown eyes open wide with appreciation. One of them took a set in his hands and checked the well-crafted leather and buckles, and another asked Perse in her language if they should mount the bridles on the horses.

"Not yet. I want Helios to see them first. Let him decide when to use them."

When Asim, the Egyptian stable master, joined them, he leaned in to examine the tawny leather and said, "Whoever made these bridles has raised horses; they are experts of the craft. I have never seen such a polished set!"

"Athenian masters crafted these specially for Helios's horses," she said, smiling.

Asim's voice pulsed with excitement, "What precious stones have they set on the brows and nosebands, my queen!" She had selected fine emeralds that glimmered on the leather straps, for she knew they would appeal to Helios's aesthetic.

"Precious stones," she repeated.

"It will take the grooms a while to adjust them for each

horse." Asim asked for the grooms' attention by calling out their names. "We don't have enough time today. Helios is prompt in his departure time."

The queen knew he was right; she dismissed her attendant and lingered with the stable hands. "What are Helios's favorite stops these days?" she asked.

"He sees his sister Selene almost every day," Asim and the groom answered in one breath.

"Sometimes he stops to see his children too," another boy offered.

"He used to take Circe for rides, when she was young," Perse mused.

The small group made room for four boys to leave the gathering and lead the horses out of the paddocks. In single file, under the stable master's discerning eye, they walked to the arena to warm up for the day's journey.

All was perfectly timed. Helios appeared, radiant, handsome, and tireless, carrying his whip and a pair of leather gloves tucked into his belt. When she heard him approach, Perse called out, "Husband, the world awaits your arrival every day, and so do I. Come, I have something special to show you."

"Perse!" He tossed his blond hair, grinned from ear to ear, and joined the gathering. She took his hand and led him to the arena, pointing to the bridles.

She watched his eyes get wide as he exclaimed, "Where did you find them?" and stepped closer to the fence. "What a fine set!" he marveled.

"A present for you," she said, expectantly.

He picked up one set and inspected it closely, silent for a moment. "Well suited for Aethon, Eous, Phlegon, and Pyrois. Such fine workmanship, and I adore the decorative gems. What are they?" He looked at Perse as he slid his fingers along the leather browband.

"Emeralds, your birthstone."

Helios handed the bridle to his stable master, who carried it back to the fence, remarking, "A perfect choice for your Lordship's horses."

"I only wish there was enough time to mount them, but that would delay my daily trek. I want to try them tomorrow," he told the stable master. His eyes locked on Perse. "It's a wonderful present for my team. Thank you."

Perse smiled. "Yes, my gift to your fiery horses. I meant it for you, but would Phaethon like it for his birthday?"

"A perfect idea. I think he will. It is time he learned how to ride horses." He moved closer to her. "Let's share a meal tonight. I want to thank you properly for the gift, for honoring the boy." Helios held his wife around her waist and pulled her in. He gave her a peck on her cheek, then turned to the grooms and ordered, "Hitch my chariot. Time to start this day." He gave her a last squeeze and whispered, "I am counting on my clever wife to come up with ways to help Selene."

The chariot was ready for him, and the stable master handed him his rayed headdress to wear. Perse adjusted it for him and suggested, "Check with the daughters you fathered with another lover. Phaethusa and Lampetia may know more about Selene. Invite them to Phaethon's celebration. They will come."

"I will. See if you can find out any more too."

She was a little disappointed that he did not delay his trek to try the new bridles. Yet after all their years of marriage, she recognized Helios's devotion to his routines and the needs of the planet, understood his responsibilities, and admired his exact timing. He kept order in the world and had the power to tilt his orbit so that he could usher in four seasons.

The boys brought the chariot around with his horses hitched, just as the moon faded on the horizon, and all was ready to begin a new day. Helios mounted the chariot and took the reins from the waiting groom.

Perse watched him lead the horses to the launch site, holding the reins loosely. It was the moment she had always enjoyed, experiencing the thrust of trotting hooves that sped up as they surged forward. He pulled the reins and snapped the whip, and the horses ramped up, leaping off the ground for takeoff. It was an alluring sight to see them gallop skyward, transcending the darkness, bringing radiance to the sky.

Perse gave the satchel and bridles to the stable master and asked him to have them delivered to her at Phaethon's birthday party. She started for the palace with Selene on her mind. She would find a way to stall a disaster. Whom should she enlist?

THREE

FAMILY MATTERS

J ust as young dawn, with her rose-red fingers, appeared on the horizon, Perse left the stables for the palace. She followed a tree-covered, well-trodden path, willing the birds to sing their morning songs. Enchanted with their trills and tweets, she rested on a bench to let Helios's warmth and sunlight wash over her. Her husband had handed her a new problem, and she had to generate ideas about who might aid her in her mission to rescue Selene. Because it was family trouble, she would send an attendant to invite her sister, Clymene, for breakfast to consider other allies.

Who would have information? Perse remembered the ancient magician, Hecate, who would naturally link to Selene. Hecate's dark moon always began the cycle of a full moon. She would have up-to-date information about her sister-in-law's trouble with Zeus. The queen knew that the goddess of sorcery and witchcraft had heightened powers at night.

She called Leonora to bring her scrying mirror from her bedroom. When she had it, she held it reverentially, raising it with both hands. Perse had inherited it from her mother, goddess Tethys, known as the mother of rain clouds, wife of the Titan Oceanus. It gave her special privileges when she invoked the goddess: immediate access to Hecate. Shaped like a full moon, the obsidian mirror reflected the shadows of the sky, and came to life with her touch. A pair of silver hands framed its perimeter, long fingers crossing its top. The handle resolved into an elegant, slim head of a snake. Perse sat on the lip of the fountain, gripping the mirror firmly, and turned toward the sky.

There was no sign of the moon when she called for Hecate. The goddess of magic and witchcraft usually answered her petitioners in the dark hours of the night, but the matter was urgent. A faint image appeared in the scrying mirror after Perse's third call, and a voice spoke faintly. "Is that you, Perse, daughter of Tethys?"

"Oh, Hecate, protector of our household, I implore you. I need your help. Selene, my dear husband's sister, has caught the ire of Zeus."

Hecate sighed, sounding annoyed. "It can wait, dear Perse. Let's rendezvous at midnight." The mirror went empty, reflecting an absence. Perse shook her head, disappointed. She set the mirror on a bench, hoping that the sorceress would eventually return with information and a plan.

Her sister was due to arrive. Perse clapped her hands and ordered the servants to set a table for their breakfast in the garden, under an arbor covered with fragrant wisteria vines. Then she returned to her bedroom and called Leonora to bring her light green tunic. "When you come back, I want your help to fix my hair the way Hera wears hers." The last time she had visited Mount Olympus, Zeus's wife wore a diadem over her shiny, perfumed locks and had her hair covered with a veil. "And bring me a few filmy veils to shield my brow. I will choose one for you to drape over my hair," she said, waving Leonora away.

She chose a pair of silver moon earrings, Selene's gift, and wore them. Then she clapped her hands again, and when a servant appeared, she had him bring the smallest parcel, a souvenir from her trip. It was a wooden box, carefully wrapped in several layers of soft cloth. She unwrapped it, set it on a trunk and, with a key she carried on a chain that hung around her delicate neck, unlocked it, and selected a small box. It contained a pair of silver water-drop earrings, a gift from her daughter Circe for Clymene.

Perse hoped to enlist the support of her daughter, sister, and niece in any action necessary to get Selene out of trouble. Clymene had been helpful in the past when family problems arose. Perhaps this time Helios would grant his women a Great Hall of their own, rewarding their services.

Clymene was escorted to the garden and settled at the table next to the fragrant wisteria trellis. It was still early morning, and a cloud of fog covered Mount Olympus. She was not an early riser but, responding to her sister's bidding, had rushed to dress in a simple white tunic. Besides, she wanted to talk with Perse about her son's birthday celebration.

Leonora interrupted her thoughts, setting a bowl of rice pudding and a pitcher of freshly squeezed pomegranate juice on the table. "Greetings. Welcome to Queen Perse's quarters. She will be here soon."

"My good woman, my sister woke me up early. I am here and she has not shown up yet! Perse is impossible," Clymene spoke, smoothing down her clothes. It was an old grudge: *Always second best in the palace when Perse is here.*

Leonora smiled and poured her a glass of pomegranate juice. "Please, have some breakfast. Don't wait for the queen. The food will get cold. How are your nieces, Phaethusa and Lampetia? Will we see them at the celebration?"

Clymene sagged back in her chair. "My nieces are on their way already. I wish Trinacia, their island, was closer. We would see them more often."

Reaching for the fresh fruit that was laid out on a platter, Clymene saw the chance to learn what the palace help chatted about. Leonora rarely disappointed.

But before Clymene could speak, the maid asked a question. "What about the mortal king, Merops of Ethiopia? Is he coming?" she inquired of Clymene, who looked away.

"I don't know that yet," answered Clymene.

She would discuss it with Perse, uncertain of how Helios would react. Besides, it was none of Leonora's business to pry. Helios had not met King Merops, the mortal who had stood by her and helped her raise Phaethon.

When Clymene had revealed to her son that Helios was his true father, the boy was ecstatic. The sun-god had invited them to live in his palace, and they soon moved in. Clymene was sad to say her goodbyes to her kind mortal companion but was lured by the advantages life with Helios could bring to their son.

During their last few weeks in Ethiopia, the boy had turned arrogant, cold, and dismissive of the kind king. "I am the son of a god," he bragged, embarrassing his mother, who considered Merops and thought fondly of his thunderous graying beard and warm brown eyes.

Leonora busied herself, taking out a dust cloth from her apron pocket and running it over the empty chairs. "Is there anything you would like me to bring you?"

"It's all good!" said Clymene. "No need to wait on me."

Leonora placed her hand on her chest, bowed, and was gone.

Clymene looked around the garden and noticed the scrying mirror lying on a bench by the fountain. Although she was a daughter of the same mother as Perse, she avoided dark sorcery. *What is she up to now?* she wondered.

Clymene had been preparing for days for her son's birthday

with the help of the palace servants, sending invitations and ordering decorations that were waiting to be installed in the Great Hall. The kitchen was preparing delicacies and had plenty of wine for the event. She hoped that both her sister and Helios would offer generous gifts and acknowledge Phaethon's place in the palace. Presently he was the sun-god's only son who lived under Helios's roof.

Clymene worried about her boy's outbursts and tantrums; he was not a baby anymore, but since everyone seemed to tolerate him, she avoided dealing with it. In the comforts of palace life, Phaethon's mother had only one ambition: to see her son rise.

She took a sip of juice, and as she was setting her glass down, Perse showed up behind the fountain, from the direction of the temple at the far end of the garden. Her sister was her usual elegant self, bejeweled, perfumed, with her perfect coiffure, her face covered by a yellow filmy veil. Clymene moved toward her to greet her, and the two women embraced.

Perse had a lot on her mind. They sat across from each other. "Are you ready for the birthday, sister?" she asked, guessing what was uppermost in Clymene's mind. "Who is coming? What are the plans? I am sorry to be a latecomer to it." She helped herself to the pudding.

"The food and decorations are nearly taken care of. I wanted your opinion about King Merops. Should I send for him?" Clymene started peeling a fig.

"Don't rub a raw wound, Clymene. It will probably be uncomfortable for Phaethon to have both fathers here at once, uncomfortable for the fathers too." Sensible Perse had responded swiftly. "I look forward to the day and hope the young people will behave with decorum. We should make sure the servants thin the wine with plenty of water. No drunken brawls like those that broke out when we celebrated your birthday!"

The queen noticed her sister bite her lip. Clymene blushed. "I will instruct the help to keep track of my son's drinking," she said, and sank her teeth into the luscious fig.

"I have a gift for you from your niece Circe." Perse handed her sister a small box. A broad, satisfied smile blossomed on Clymene's face.

"My dear niece! She has not forgotten me!" She opened the box and took out the pair of silver water-drop earrings. "We all are daughters of the ocean. I love it! When did you see her last?"

"Right before I returned to the palace. She was planning a three-day festival for her people with events honoring the muses. There are some fabulous musicians, poets, and thespians on Aeaea. I wanted to attend, but Helios finally summoned me."

"When will you see her next? I, too, have a gift for her." Clymene asked for a mirror, and when Leonora brought it, she replaced her earrings with the new pair. "Pretty," she said approvingly.

"You always got along with my daughter better than I did, Clymene." Perse looked at her sister pursing her lips. "I am trying to be a better mother."

"You were strict with her. But it's never too late," Clymene said kindly.

"It is how we were taught. Our mother, Tethys, with her wise, winged forehead, often frowned on me. She was highly disciplined and had high expectations. I am still most like her, Clymene. I like to be in charge, solve problems, and refuse to be subservient to others. Our mother in her way loved us, and she loves Circe."

"Yes, she loves all her grandchildren. I still see her in my sleep, her dark eyes, her long dark hair, parted in the middle," sighed Clymene. "Next time when I visit, come with me. She will be glad to see you after all these decades."

Perse looked away and changed the subject. "I was at the temple earlier and offered a sacrifice to Hera, asking for her protection of our family and especially Phaethon! Queen Hera listens and understands women's heartaches." Perse served her sister more pudding.

"Blessings to you, Perse. I understand you want Fates to treat Phaethon well. He is still young."

"My dear sister, we all love and want more for our children. I also shared with the Olympian Hera our worries about Selene. Did you know she is in trouble with Zeus?"

"I heard Helios was spending more time with her recently, but that was not the reason. What is it?" Clymene swallowed another spoonful of pudding.

"What I have learned is that she is in love with a mortal, and Zeus is angry with them. I hope Hecate knows more. I will need your help to plan a way to stall disasters."

Clymene bristled. "Helios needs our help again! I will help you, Perse, but I am tired of him. He asks all the time. He should take care of his troubles himself. I have enough to worry about with my son." She took a couple more bites and set her bowl on the table.

Perse had hoped for a better reception. "Just this once, my dear sister. Tonight I hope to hear more about this situation from Hecate." The women fell silent and finished their breakfast. When the queen clapped her hands, Leonora appeared with a slave in tow to clear the table.

Perse turned to Clymene again. "I want to make sure my nephew has the protection of Olympian gods for life. Helios is there to watch after him during the day, but I think we should solicit Selene's favors for the dark hours of the night. The moon is a powerful presence, and Selene's light and wisdom are an important ally. Phaethon is young, a time when risk-taking is high and judgment is rushed and not always sound."

Clymene nodded. "He could use help and protection. I expect him back from his first hunting outing." She looked at Perse directly and cleared her throat. "You can count on me, Perse."

They both had busy days ahead. Clymene left the arbor first, followed by her escort, who had been waiting at a respectable distance to give the sisters privacy.

Wending her way through the garden, Perse called out, "Let me know when you need my help."

FOUR

RETURN FROM THE HUNT

*I*n the early afternoon, a group of young men were returning to the palace from the farthest reaches of the forest. It was a noisy, dusty crew retracing their steps home after taking part in their first hunt. Their leather quivers were nearly empty, suspended on their backs with bows and a few arrows.

During the hunt, their instructor had paired them to stay close and track each other for safety. Phaethon's companion was Orion, a lanky boy, the oldest and most accomplished in archery. He was mild-mannered, athletic, and got along with most everyone. Until then, no one had confronted Phaethon for his poor skills, abrupt manner, and awkwardness, and Helios's son hated failure and criticism. He hated it so much that he often made up imaginary accomplishments to fill the void he felt.

"Empty-handed again?" Orion, the handsome son of Kriton, shot the question to Phaethon, moving alongside him.

Another boy in back of them taunted, "Most of your arrows are gone, but you have nothing to show for it, Phaethon."

A handful of boisterous friends behind them made their

way up the terraced hill. Some had empty quivers, and several carried small game. Artemis, the goddess of the hunt, had been kind to the young boys on their first foray into the forest.

Ahead of them all was a short, athletic man from Crete, their leader and archery teacher, who had organized the hunt. He had first trained the boys to aim and shoot at the valley range, weeks before, and then led them for four days of hunting and learning how to survive in nature. All youths carried knives, bows, and arrows they had built themselves, as well as those their fathers had given them. A pack of dogs wove their way around them, lifting their noses in the damp air of the forest and howling excitedly.

Orion carried a good-sized cottontail rabbit, hanging from a sling he held over his shoulder. He had tracked it, foraging in the brambles. Then quick as lightning and quiet as a lizard, he had taken aim and had his first kill. The dogs howled, ran, and brought it back to Orion, who was soon surrounded by his friends and their teacher, praising him for his newfound success.

Phaethon's intensity vein had popped up in the center of his forehead, the same one that usually betrayed his anger and envy for his friends. Helios's son did not join the others; he just glared at Orion. The group was moving on toward the palace when Phaethon slipped, fell on the ground, and scuffed his knee on a sharp rock. They all stopped and huddled around him. He sat up to examine the wound that was turning red. Then he scowled at his companion, sprang to his feet, and yelled, "You tripped me!"

Orion smiled. "You are clumsy," he said, stepping closer and extending a helping hand.

Phaethon did not know what uncoiled inside him in moments like that. His friend's words tore into him. His wounded pride released in him a blind fury. In seconds, his free fist had landed on Orion's face and the pair was wrestling in the dirt.

The circle widened around them as the boys watched the struggle. Phaethon had pinned his friend down when their Cretan instructor intervened and pulled them apart. Helios's son was still breathing heavily and started dusting his clothes when he heard a couple of the boys exclaim disapprovingly, "What did you do?" and then, "You are bleeding!"

Phaethon leaned against an old oak tree to check his knee. A small rock had broken the skin and was still embedded in his flesh. He flicked it away and watched the blood trickle down. Then he saw Orion leap to his feet and shout, pointing to the ground, "You tripped on this boulder . . . I did not trip you . . . Too busy glowering at me?"

"No one talks to me like that," flared Phaethon, lunging at his companion, but this time the teacher was ready. He trapped the angry boy from behind with his muscular arms and in a firm voice ordered, "Enough!" It was not Phaethon's first tantrum.

The rest of the huddle hesitated for a moment and then moved toward the palace, leaving the three men behind. When Phaethon stopped struggling to get free, their instructor released him. Helios's son rubbed his temples as Orion turned his back on him and left for the palace. The teacher dusted off the boy and leaned over his knee. "It is a superficial wound. Tie a clean cloth over it and the bleeding will stop soon." Then he patted the boy on the back and offered, "Do you want to meet me at the range tomorrow? We can practice, so that you can perfect your aim."

"Just don't tell my mother about this. She is already upset about the death of a mortal, Icarus."

His teacher looked confused. "Who is Icarus?"

"He is the son of the master craftsman Daedalus. Icarus plunged to his death in the sea when his wings, made of feathers and wax, were melted by the heat of the sun. I wonder if my father did it on purpose." He bit his lip, realizing what suspicion had just escaped his lips, and hastened away from his teacher, calling out, "Anyway, I will meet you at noon."

Phaethon had a tender spot for Clymene. Right then, he could imagine her eyes filled with care and worry. Proud Phaethon wanted to keep his problems to himself, but he knew she was an endless snoop when it came to him. He hoped she would not find out.

The sound of yelping dogs drew Clymene to her study window. They interrupted her efforts to put words down on the page to draft a new poem. The boys were chattering merrily as they approached the palace, but Phaethon lagged behind the huddle. She tidied up the pile of papers and hurried out to meet the young hunters. Together with Helios, she had handpicked young men from select families, inviting them to attend archery lessons and other activities with Phaethon, and this was their first outing.

She ran down the steps and outside the palace to meet her son and his friends. Even from a distance, she could see that he seemed grumpy. She noticed his bleeding knee right away. "Are you hurt, Phaethon?"

She was already examining the wound when he answered, frowning, "I am fine. I just need to clean up."

Right behind him was the archery instructor. Clymene turned and, smiling, she asked the teacher, "How was the hunt? Did the boys enjoy it?"

"They did. Your son did well. He is making progress in his archery skills. Next time I expect he will bring you some game." He bowed slightly and walked past mother and son, leaving them alone.

"Let's go to your room where you can rest and place your foot high to stop the bleeding. How did this happen?" Although concerned, she kept her voice level.

The boy answered immediately. "My friend Orion tripped me for a joke. They all think I am clumsy; I fell and all they could do was mock me, Mother. I am better than any of them. I am the son of Helios!"

"I am sure they know who you are," she replied calmly. "I understand Orion is very nice and skilled in archery already. He wouldn't hurt you."

"Thinks he is important! I will prove him wrong after my birthday, when I ride a chariot and bring the light of day to the world. He may be better at archery, but I will be more important riding my father's horses."

Clymene was silent, surprised by her son's jealousy. In his bedroom, she had him place his leg on a stool, bandaged his knee, and reassured him, "Fortunately, it's superficial." She perceived Phaethon was enjoying her ministrations and took more time cleaning his muddy leg.

"How is my birthday party coming along, Mother?" he asked.

"We will be all ready for you. Have you considered what gifts you might ask for from your father?"

"I know what I want. I am his son. He should let me ride his chariot and bring the sunshine to the world for a day. Do you think he will?"

Clymene sighed. "I would think of something else too. You cannot predict what Helios will do. Besides, I don't believe it's a good idea, my son. He would do a lot for you, but it is his horses I worry about. He is their master; they know and accept his commands, but they do not recognize you. They are difficult to manage. Merops was training you in trade and the economy, for his country dealt with exporting maize, wheat, myrrh, and other incenses. Helios raises his sons following the Greek philosophy. He wants a healthy mind to live in a healthy body and is helping you to improve what mattered little to Merops."

His answer worried her that he had not yet overcome his bad temper. "I cannot," he insisted, "think of something else right now." He seemed to hesitate and startled her when he asked, "Mother, why did my father kill Icarus?"

Clymene blinked, alarmed that Phaethon had twisted the news. "It's a long, heartbreaking story, my son; we heard the news from sailors that came from Icaria last week. I confess, I shed tears hearing it, for he was your age. Another needless death, but it was not your father's fault, not his intention." She wanted to scold him for that thought, but covered her mouth momentarily, cleared her voice, and continued calmly. "Icarus's father had finished building a labyrinth in Crete for the palace and was ready to leave the island with his son, but the king of Crete wanted to keep him in his service and had him and his son confined." She shook her head disapprovingly. "Minos can be a harsh, demanding ruler. To escape, Daedalus built two sets of wings."

"I know, Mother," he interrupted her, but Clymene wanted him to hear the entire story.

"He made one set for himself and another for his son, out of feathers and beeswax. He warned Icarus to fly low and avoid the strong rays of the sun and the foam of the sea, but the boy ignored his father's guidance and flew high. The tragedy, my son, is that the beeswax melted in the sun's heat, and the boy fell to his death near a remote Aegean island. His father is burying him there. It breaks my heart. So young and, no doubt, well loved." She noticed Phaethon nodded and leaned to examine his knee.

"If only he had listened . . ." She checked to see if she had made any impact. Phaethon was looking out of the window. *The invulnerability of youth*, she thought, discouraged. She handed him a clean cloth that he took and set beside him. *I hope I have dispelled his fears about his father.*

Clymene watched servants arrive and light the torches and oil lamps in Phaethon's room, and one of them announced that his bath was drawn. Phaethon got up, and Clymene bade him goodnight. "I will see you tomorrow, once you have rested," she said, her smile sagging, and left the room. On her way to her rooms, Clymene contemplated seeking her sister's council about her son's demand and making sure her sister knew the Daedalus and Icarus story. Would Perse help her with Phaethon?

FIVE

SELENE'S LOVER

W hen her chariot landed at the mouth of the cave, Selene dismounted and settled the pair of winged steeds, spreading out mounds of barley, harnessing water from the clouds, and leaving them to feed and drink from the dimples on the ground. She called for Endymion and, getting no response, moved inside, spreading her gentle pale light around the dark walls. "Dear Endymion, it is our time, my love," she said adoringly, still searching for him.

The sheep had settled for the night in a far corner of the cave. The goddess found her lover sprawled out next to a spilled cup of wine, snoring loudly, lying on lambswool sheepskins. Approaching, she parted his golden locks and leaned over to kiss him. He always kept himself clean and combed, but tonight she could smell it again. The fumes of alcohol emanated from his breath. Momentary anger coursed through her body. *Not again. It has been several days in a row.* The goddess felt her throat throbbing, upset with the reign of red wine and the stained sheepskins. What was the matter with him? What did her brother think of this situation?

Helios had greeted her in his usual way earlier in the in-between space of their time shifts. "I am turning over the rest of the hours to you, dear Selene." Then he lingered. "But I am worried about you," he went on, and as he guided his chariot to follow the usual path to his palace, he said, "Zeus is angry with all of us."

"I cannot help myself, dear brother. It will work out," she answered with a helpless smile, her silver bracelets jingling as she pulled the reins to stop her steeds. This was more than their daily exchange, although recently she had slipped and shared, "He likes his drink." The thought had crossed her addled mind to reconsider this relationship and even leave him. However, she had seen Zeus's eyebrows raised and his face turn severe, threatening a tantrum. She knew that her mother and father thought the mortal shepherd was becoming her alluring tyrant. Where was her will to shake him up or even abandon him? Yet this lover had awakened her desire, her sensual instincts, and given her so many nights of heavenly bliss! Was it an addiction?

She approached Endymion, lightly touched his face, shook him, and watched him open his blue-gray eyes slowly. He was a handsome man, his muscular body inviting, still warm from sleep. She watched him stretch his arms. She loved those eyes and his smile of recognition when he looked at her. But how much had he drunk again tonight? He reached out and affectionately brushed her cheek, his smile blinding her again. "My dear, you fell asleep and spilled your wine. How much did you drink?" she said, crouching next to him.

"How much did I drink," he growled, rubbing his eyes. Then he shifted to a sweeter tone and said, "My dear love, I missed you. Don't you know I love you?"

Biting down on her lip, she took his hand and pulled him up to a sitting position. "I don't want you in this condition. It has been too many nights already," she scolded him, knitting her eyebrows.

"I am not a young man. At forty, I need my sleep, my dear."

She pulled back a little when he reached for her cheeks; she had spread silver glitter just for him tonight.

"You are my beautiful goddess, my woman."

He left her side, got up, and walked out of the cave, mumbling, "I will be a minute." She could hear his endless stream of pee, emptying what he had consumed. Her noisy steeds that had been feeding peacefully outside let out loud neighs.

Back inside, Endymion protested, "Your beauties will wake up my sheep." The herd—his one hundred sheep—stirred but did not become agitated. "My lovely, you are worth all the trouble in the world!" he added, settling back.

She felt his eyes undressing her. He made her feel like his queen. He knew all the special spots on her body that already tingled with anticipation. She loved his round eyes and his tan body. When he played love tunes with his pipes, he mesmerized her; he knew so many haunting mountain melodies.

Selene thought he loved her plenty, but all these years later, she wondered if he was getting bored with her, turning to wine and maybe to other women to fill his days. She had selected a blue light silk tunic and was wearing the perfume he had once told her he loved. She had sprayed it on her chest and dabbed it behind her ears before she left her palace. For his sake, she was at odds with her brother. Zeus was getting impatient with her. The pressure was mounting.

When he settled down on the sheepskin, he came close to her and whispered in her ear, "You look so divine tonight." She felt his hungry hands reach for her, and shivers swept through her body. She turned, looked at him, and said, batting her eyes, "What do you want from me, my dear?"

"I want you, all of you, my beauty. Every inch!" She lay down, and he moved closer, kissing her breasts.

She let him remove her tunic, and they sank into each other. He was a gifted lover. He knew all the ways to coax and give her pleasures she had not known with anyone else. It was another sweet night, even with the wine-scenting of his breath.

With her passion satiated, she kissed his eyes and moved away to dress. "Till tomorrow, dear Endymion," she said, but truly wished to stay with him for all eternity. He seemed so genuine in his affections for her tonight.

"I need to be at the village tomorrow to get feeding supplies for my lambs and will have to stay overnight," he said, looking outside the cave. "The weather is pleasant now, but it will not last forever. I want to take care of my flock."

Was there an actual need? It was still spring and there was plenty for the sheep to graze, roaming on hillsides during the day. "Then I will see you in a couple of nights," she said, her voice sounding hollow.

Sometimes she wondered if he could read her mind as he moved into what had become his frequent call for action. "You say you love me, but you will not have me forever. You know, all men's days are numbered." And then, "You keep promising and stalling. When will you give me the precious gift of immortality?"

His hints were frequent and were becoming oppressive. Selene moved away from him. "Only Zeus can grant this gift to you. All I can do is ask." Selene knew that the father of all gods had favored her in past years but had soured watching her affair with this mortal. Still, being a gifted dreamer, she hoped that with persistence, Zeus would grant her wish to give Endymion immortality. But there were moments when she feared the day her shepherd would get his wish. *What if he abandons me once he gains immortality? Look at Zeus and my brother, Helios. They love their adventures with women.*

But the distant future was always a little hazy to see in her dreams. And she wanted to be with him tomorrow night and the night after.

At Helios's palace, few knew about Selene's affair on faraway Mount Latmus besides Perse and Clymene, Zeus, and the night sky. On the day before the birthday party, Perse lingered, watching the rise of the moon. She had often marveled over her husband's harmonious relationships with his two sisters, Selene and Eos. They each handed off their part in the twenty-four-hour dance gently to the other. Eos, the personification of dawn, was the quiet sister who kept to herself. Occasionally, Perse would visit with her sister-in-law. Helios's wife loved the quiet hours of dawn and from time to time had shared her innermost thoughts with her sister-in-law, who possessed a wisdom she respected. Dawn was a gentle and wise goddess. Perse held her ivory wand and pointed it to the horizon line, concentrating on inviting Eos who usually responded just after handing her reign to Helios.

Before the rooster's crow, Perse sat by her window facing the garden. Soon Eos appeared from the direction of the temple. She wore a simple tunic belted with a silver chain and walked in silver sandals, elegant in her simplicity. She greeted Perse respectfully, "Hello, my queen!"

"You came," said Perse, relieved. "I need your insights about how to help Selene."

"My sister is beginning to get disenchanted with Endymion, dear Perse. The last time we talked about him, this slipped past her lips: 'I don't like it when I find him drinking. Is he womanizing?'"

Perse was intrigued. "A good development. I don't understand how Endymion has lured her."

"He's not a good companion for Selene. Our parents are concerned," Eos said, settling on the grass beyond the window, and Perse joined her outside. "I think of late Selene has got an accurate picture of the man."

"Does she confide in you?"

Eos tilted back her head, sharing a playful grin. "We talk every day, when she hands me the balance of the hours and I take over from her. I have an idea that might work. What if she asked Zeus to give him immortality but place him in a lingering state of sleep? That way, he would be at her disposal but unavailable to do more womanizing?"

Perse was intrigued. *This might work. An excellent compromise.* She said, "Do you think Zeus would settle for that?"

Eos went on, "I believe it would be easier for the gods to tolerate his existence, even his immortality, if he remained inactive and unobtrusive."

The more Perse thought about Eos's suggestion, the more it made sense to her. *Besides, if Zeus accepts this solution, in time Selene might get over her infatuation,* she thought. She knew that the father of all gods was no model himself, but he liked Selene.

"It just might work," Eos said. "Think about it. Talk to my brother." She had nothing more to add and moved away. "Enjoy the day, dear Perse," she said, fading into the sky.

Eager to follow Eos's proposal, Perse returned to her bed and listened for her husband's arrival.

Each dawn, when Helios finished his daily run, he would often come directly from the stables to his room to clean up and relax. He had trained the servants not to bother him after his bath. Just as he was settling on his fur-lined chair, he recognized his wife's approaching footsteps. Perse crossed a short corridor to his adjoining rooms, lifted the arras, and settled on another chair by him. "Have you any news from Selene?"

He had, of course, seen his sister when they changed the guard, but he told Perse that Selene was cautious. She had not shared any worries openly. Instead, today she had asked him about Phaethon's birthday, stating that she was sending him a gift she hopes he likes.

"What is it?" he had asked, holding his team of horses a minute longer.

"A shield that will protect him in battle," Selene had answered. "I hope he never has to go to war, but if he does, it has the magic touch of Hephaistos, the god of fire, a craftsman like no other, and will protect him well."

"It is perfect for this young man," Perse said now, brushing a curl from her forehead. "I am sure he will like it." Then she changed the subject. "Did you meet with Hera?"

He looked away when she pressed him again. "She was pleased to see me stop to greet her, but I don't think she will come. She did say she would send a present for Phaethon."

"You see the damage of your stubborn refusal. If I had a proper place to host her, her answer would be different, dear husband!" she scoffed. "I, too, have news to share, but only if you promise to build me my Great Hall. I have a plan."

"I knew you would come up with something." He smiled, shaking his head, as she ticked off the advantages of her plan.

Perse was on a roll. "It resolves the bind Selene has put us in. It will help our relationship with Zeus and, in time, free Selene from the charms of Endymion. You have to promise me that when I have succeeded, you will build the new wing that gives me a Great Hall to invite goddesses and hold assemblies."

It was a lure she thought would work.

"Not so fast, my dear. Tell me your plan."

"First your word, and then I will start taking action. You can put this worry out of your mind. But I will do nothing unless I get a promise!"

"So, how will you solve this?"

"Trust me. I know Selene's state of mind and Zeus's dilemma.

I have a compromise that will resolve their issues and please them both. Have some faith, my husband!"

"Pray tell me what you have in mind, and I can judge if the price is right."

"The price is right. You will not deliver unless I succeed," she answered confidently, taking his hands in hers and looking him in the eye.

Helios had seen her many successes; he knew she was capable. She had proven it many times, but still he pushed for a disclosure. After more wrangling, he realized that his wife would not share her plan.

"You know I will succeed!" she said proudly. "I will prepare a special perfume for your sister. Will you take it to her? It is a thank-you for her present to my nephew."

"A perfect response. I am sure she will appreciate it, Perse. As for the Great Hall you have been pressing for: I will build it only if you deliver, and if Zeus, Selene, and I are satisfied." For Selene's sake, he conceded.

Triumphant, she kissed him, called his servant, and ordered some fruit to share and celebrate her win. "It will revive us," she said. "Come to the garden to see the rising moon and enjoy the night."

SIX

HERA AND PERSE'S PERFUMES

*T*he next evening, Perse returned to the same corner of the garden where she had shared breakfast with Clymene, carrying the mirror by her side. Impatient, she started pacing, waiting for divine Hecate to appear.

When Leonora appeared to check on her mistress, and to pass the time, Perse began reminiscing, "Do you remember the time Hera stopped at Helios's palace?" She knew her maid would remember the queen of gods and wife/sister of Zeus.

Leonora answered, "How could I forget hearing about it from my mother! It was a special occasion! She arrived here, preceded by goddess Iris, her youthful messenger, traveling on the rainbow road laid out for her. Mother told me that Hera's chariot was pulled by peacocks and came in time to bless your centennial wedding anniversary with Helios!"

"It was not the only time she favored us. There was an earlier time when she descended from Mount Olympus. That was before your time with me. I had a difficult pregnancy with Circe that continued for two weeks beyond my full term. I was worried that my baby might be dead. As the delivery was getting delayed, I offered a sacrifice of ten cows to glorious Hera, who responded right away."

"She came?" marveled Leonora, her eyes open wide, her lips slightly parted.

"Iris came first to announce her arrival to Helios. Hera came to the palace carried by her gorgeous peacocks and found me in the birthing room in labor. She sat by the doorway, breathing calm and ease into the room. I delivered a healthy baby in the next hour under her protection. She is my majestic ally and champion, always preceded by Iris's rainbows."

"Well deserved, my queen. Olympians honor you, for you come from Titan royal stock."

"I belong with the mighty goddesses who grace Mount Olympus, dear Leonora. But enough of that. I have a message for Circe; bring me a carrier pigeon. I need to let her know I will miss the festival on her island but will see her soon." Perse turned, checked the scrying mirror, and dismissed her.

It was still dusk when the obsidian shadows parted. Even before the goddess of witchcraft and sorcery appeared, Perse could feel her vibration overtaking the space around her. Then Hecate's face filled the mirror, crone wrinkles around her eyes projecting kindness and wisdom. A grateful Perse uttered, "Divine Hecate!"

The goddess met her eyes with a wide grin. "It's not so bad, sister. Zeus is putting pressure on your husband, but he is fond of Selene. He will accept a compromise." Perse grew unusually quiet and listened carefully to Hecate, who lowered her voice and said, "I know Helios loves high drama."

Drawing her eyebrows together, Perse asked, "How urgent is this? Do we have some time?"

Hecate cackled, "No rush! It can wait until after Phaethon's birthday party."

"What is Zeus upset about?"

The question appeared to put the goddess in a gossipy mood. "Helios's sister is bedding down a shepherd, a mere mortal. Mortals who have affairs with gods anger Zeus, but this man is pressing Selene to gain immortality for himself. Helios has ample time to deal with it."

Although reassured that there was no press for time, Perse drummed her fingers on the table, worried about needing to deal with Helios's anxiety in another hour. "Do I need to help resolve his panic? Would Hera help me out?" Perse leaned into the mirror to listen carefully.

"She is wise and would side with us; she could suggest a reasonable way to keep everyone satisfied. However, it would be best if you visited her yourself, dear Perse. Make another offering, invite her to the party. If she refuses, approach her at the mountain."

"Always grateful for your advice. I will dispatch a pigeon with an invitation to the party right away."

The mirror went dark, and Perse clapped her hands twice for Leonora. Perse could not help but feel excitement about the prospect of engaging Hera. She trusted that Helios would like that as well.

In the predawn, her husband's words came to Perse—his fear of Zeus's anger and punishment, how he begged her to devise ways to avoid disaster, and his final words: "Time is short, but you are clever, Perse."

Worried, she rose from her bed, thinking, *I must act now*, and moved at once to her special room where she plied her skills in creating perfumes. She made sure Leonora was not nearby before sitting at a wide table littered with hundreds of clear and colored glass and ceramic vials, her impressive arsenal. She was known for mastering the alchemy and the craft of creating perfume blends that had special properties. Her methodical groupings clustered all rainbow colors, designs and shapes, her secret way to classify them. She had droppers, spoons, cups, and a distillery set up next to her table.

Perse was convinced that Leonora spied on her special room on the second floor, and knew that red vials marked poisons, yellow ones were innocent, sweet and spicy, and blue represented her mistress's ancestry from the sea. Several gods and mortals had enjoyed riding on her magic and mysterious carpet of scents. Aphrodite regularly ordered a supply to gift to her maidens, who were sure to trap lovers into their web. On special request, she had delivered preparations that could suppress erotic urges too.

But there was much more to this art. Perse had helped the Egyptians to empty corpses of their organs and fill their cavities with preservatives and aromatics to prepare them for the afterlife. She had mastered secrets of manufacturing blends and knew how to assign spells. Perse's perfumes were fun, sensual, dangerous, and visceral—and a few had magic properties.

Surveying her collection of essential oils, she realized that she was almost out of patchouli. She needed to replenish some ingredients. The gardeners would have to collect leaves and stems from parent plants, harvest and dry them, then prepare a distillation for her collection. They were her source for roots, wildflowers, and woods, and she relied on them to make special preparations for her.

She made a list of what she needed and then came downstairs and walked away from the palace. The view was of cultivated fields, separated by rows of trees. She took the uphill path under a shadowy canopy of trees that led to the gardening center. Luscious ferns draped over mulch had branched out all around the gardener's hut. Her sandals crunched on the ground. She could hear laughter inside.

A man spoke, "Rumor has it that she had fifty children with the shepherd."

Are they gossiping about Selene?

"Lucky shepherd!" another said in low tones, snickering. "Perhaps she is a nymphomaniac!" A round of loud giggles followed his remarks.

"Not unlike you!" came a retort.

Entering, Perse could not suppress her own laughter. She pulled the door wide open and found four people working on the counters, filling pots with dirt and sowing seeds.

"It isn't funny. Even goddesses cannot avoid the pains of labor," answered a woman who had not yet noticed the queen. Then all hands got busy and talking ceased.

Perse pretended not to hear their conversation and handed her list to the woman. "Here is what I need you to prepare. I need all of it the soonest possible. Look into storage. You should have some dried leaves, bark, and some of the other ingredients. I need it in four days."

"My mistress, at your service," answered the woman. She removed her gloves and examined the list.

"I will count on you to bring me these products."

"Yes, my queen. Right away," the woman replied, taking a slight bow.

Turning around, Perse left the hut, smiling to herself, still amused by their conversation. They were right! Her plan was to prepare a special perfume for Selene as soon as the new ingredients were delivered.

SEVEN

PARTY GIFTS

*B*efore the rosy break of dawn, Phaethon, too excited to sleep, carried a torch through the palace hallways to pay one of his occasional visits to the stables. He had not seen his father since before the hunt and was seeking him out. The daily commotion of feeding and grooming horses was already in progress before Helios's arrival. The boy walked past the stables. A fine-looking Arabian gelding, the pride of the Bedouins, was getting groomed in a paddock. He stopped to watch, struck by its gleaming chestnut coat, its finely chiseled body and nobility. "What is his name?" he asked the groom.

"Aethon, master," said the young man just as the horse swished his tail and set his ears back. The groom spoke to the horse softly and continued brushing him.

Phaethon lingered, imagining himself mounting Aethon. With a commanding voice he ordered, "I want to ride him for a short time since Father is not here yet. Step aside."

Asim, the stable master, who was nearby, pursed his lips. "He does not know you, master. He might toss you off his back. The boy is almost done brushing him, and your father is due to arrive any time."

Helios's son, insulted by the man's insolence, stared back at him as he approached the horse and said abruptly, "Get a bridle and a pad." To himself, he thought, *I might have taken this insult before, when I believed my father to be a mortal king, but no more! I am Helios's son!*

Stepping back, the young groom said wearily, "But he does not know you, master!"

Phaethon took the brush from the boy's hands and sent him away, pointing the way to the tack room. Trying to copy the groom's circular motion, he watched the horse tense up when he brushed his coat; the animal flared his nostrils and turned his eyes wide.

Asim came back with a pad and bridles and set them on the ground. He calmly patted the horse, offering him a handful of barley. Phaethon tossed the brush to the ground and walked toward the arena where the other horses of Helios's team were already loose, trotting around, getting ready for their daily trek. "Call me when Aethon is ready!" he shouted back to the stable master.

Phaethon noticed Perse's new set of bridles still hanging on the fence. He asked Asim, who was getting ready to lead Aethon to the arena, "Are these new?"

"Yes, they are," the sun-god answered him, approaching from behind. "Do you like them?"

His son had not realized that Helios was nearby. He nodded with admiration, touching the bridles lightly. "Very special, very fine. Good day to you, Father."

"Dear Phaethon, it's your day, your celebration! I have not seen you since the hunt. How was it?" Helios asked him.

Asim handed Helios's crown to the sun-god, who took it and placed it over his blond curls.

Phaethon followed the crown with his eyes. "Dear Father, I have a lot to learn yet about hunting, but I managed to bring a cottontail rabbit home."

Helios patted him on the back. "Your mother must be proud!"

"It's small game. I was hoping to bring something larger; I did not share much with her," Phaethon said, nearly regretting his lie.

Helios smiled. "Of course, she will be proud. You must tell her! A good start, my son! It took me several hunts before I could bring any game home."

The boy hoped his small deception would remain undetected, and quickly changed the subject. "Today is my big day. My celebration! Is there time to ride Aethon for a little while?"

"You can, after Asim gives you lessons. Why don't you ride Blaze instead? He is a fine horse." Helios turned to the stable master and called out the usual morning order: "Hitch my team. I don't want to be late." Turning to Phaethon and then Asim, he continued, "You can start working with my son tomorrow. Teach him safety. Teach him well."

Asim took a slight bow. Helios winked at him. "Phaethon is in a rush to ride my team, but he needs to take it slow."

"Will you join us tonight for my celebration when you return to the palace?" Phaethon asked.

"As soon as I am back." Helios moved into the arena and added, "By now, my daughters, Phaethusa and Lampetia, have arrived at the palace for your celebration. Go and greet them."

Phaethon had not believe these guests would attend his celebration, though Clymene had told him already that they were expected any time. He was pleased and realized that his father knew most everything that transpired on the earth among gods, demigods, nymphs, and mortals as he patrolled the globe during daylight hours and had many connections.

"Glad they are here, Father. I am pleased they came." Then he rushed to ask for the special favor. "One more thing."

Helios perked up and playfully asked his son, "And what would that be?"

"I am your humble son and have a special wish for my birthday." He set his eyes on Helios's crown again. "I want to ride your chariot tomorrow for the day, rise and set the sun to the world. Will you let me relieve you for just one day? It is not too much to ask!"

Helios took a step back and in a firm voice said, "Dear son, I would like to have you ask for another gift, one that I can give you without worrying about your safety. My four horses, my beauties, they do not take kindly to a new master. Pyrois is my fiery one. Eous can take sudden turns, and Aethon blazes on the trek on his own sometimes. Even with me riding, Phlegon can set small fires on his way. We have worked together for eons—that is why they obey me. Be patient. Let the stable master teach you. You can learn and practice now and prepare for such a ride next year."

"But Father, it will only be for a day!" Phaethon persisted, pouting.

"My son, I urge you to think of something else. Asim will give you lessons. He is a master teacher. Mind him. You have all day to come up with another wish for tonight. Clymene can help you." He signaled for the grooms to finish hitching the team. "I have to start sprinkling morning light over the earth, but I will join your celebration tonight!" he reassured his son.

Phaethon watched Helios climb onto the chariot. Leaning slightly forward, his father called out to his horses, "Get up . . ." and the team leaped to the sky like the wind.

Helios's son took the long way back to the palace, striding through the halls dark and angry. Kicking the walls, he smashed a couple of terra-cotta flowerpots and mumbled angrily, "What kind of father would refuse me a favor on my birthday?" He sought refuge in his quarters, away from people to recover from the disappointment.

In his second-floor bedroom, he found family gifts delivered from close relatives, as was customary. Phaethusa and Lampetia had delivered a pair of thick woolen carpets with beautiful patterns, already lying on the marble floor, a welcome present that he guessed was woven using fibers that came from Helios's cattle. He loosened the belt around his tunic, took his sandals off, and walked with bare feet, enjoying the soft, even pile.

It picked up his mood even more to see a shiny shield lying on his bed. He rushed to examine the golden images that decorated its surface in relief. Starting from the center and moving outward, a craftsman had placed an image of Helios in the center, surrounded by symbols of twelve houses. A row of galaxies and stars followed, and on the outer edge a lineup of longhorn cattle. He felt the sculpted images with his fingers, cool to the touch and finely detailed. Noticing a note drop to the floor, he picked it up. It read, *For your protection in days of battle. May you never need to use it.* It was signed with the unmistakable mark of a crescent moon—the mark of his aunt Selene.

Next to it lay a long spear, about ten feet in length, its wooden shaft smooth and gilded, ending in a sharp iron tip. A note pierced near the tip read, *For your protection, dear Phaethon. Eos.* He smiled to himself, realizing that with their gifts, his aunts acknowledged him and marked his coming of age to practice the arts of war.

Having grown up in Ethiopia, he was not used to having attention from family, receiving presents. After his father's refusal to grant him the favor, it soothed his wounded ego to find such special gifts. Still, he had lived with his real father, Helios, for only two years and felt out of place, like a newcomer. He picked up the shield. It was heavy. His muscles twitched, lifting it, but he held it up and marched around the room with open strides. Then he took the spear and pretended to attack an invisible enemy.

The day was turning out better already. He placed the weapons against the wall and called his servant to help him put on his ornate sunburst belt over a royal-blue tunic. To finish the dress, the servant brought him a golden armband and several bracelets he was given in Ethiopia, decorated with copper inlaid meanders. Phaethon chose a plain armband and checked his image in a mirror. Standing straight, with a bulging-out chest, he was ready to face the world.

Soon all those arriving would admire the halls and the decorations for his special evening. There was a spring to his step when he arrived at the Great Hall, where he found Clymene with Phaethusa and Lampetia. His cousins had come to celebrate him from their faraway island and were already dressed for the occasion in their finery, in golden tunics, fashionable sandals with straps reaching their knees, sunburst earrings with their long hair unfolding loose with blonde highlights. They were a mirror image of each other and were teetering with excitement when they saw their cousin. The three embraced, greeting each other warmly. He thanked them for the Persian carpets specially designed for him in rich blue, green, yellow motifs and meander borders. They told him that the images represented the four seasons.

He looked around the Great Hall and twirled around with dancing steps. Servants had been working for a couple of days. The space had been richly decorated with every column festooned with blue ribbons and banners that hung between them. Signs wishing Phaethon a long, heroic life and a bright future were pinned around the walls. Local artists had created enameled copper sunbursts that covered the ceiling. Palace gardeners had collected and arranged dozens of hydrangea bouquets in cobalt-blue vases placed on short columns around the hall.

In the kitchen, preparations had been feverish for an entire week. Master chefs were at work, making sure all supplies had been brought up from the cellars under the Great Hall. The cooks had been chopping, washing, cooking, and baking food to perfection in the past three days. Aromas of delectable appetizers and complicated menus penetrated the palace. The cellars had been opened to bring up wines, and four crates were placed in the hall for easy access to those assigned the duty to replenish everybody's cylices.

Phaethon turned to his mother, feeling his heart expand with appreciation. "It's beautifully decorated, thanks to you, Mother!"

Clymene smiled. "It should be a day to remember, dear." She reminded her son that Helios had asked him to give his first public speech that evening. It was to be a speech of passage, a chance to declare his aspirations and devotion to the Olympians and his family.

The carpenters had just finished their hammering and were collecting their tools, ready to leave the hall. Following Helios's instructions, they had completed a raised stage in the middle of the Great Hall. Without hesitation, Phaethon climbed onto the dais and looked around the room; with a grand gesture as if greeting the imaginary crowd, he started, "Honored guests, may I have your attention."

He was ready to leave the dais when his cousins, curious, encouraged him, "Please, take a moment to rehearse your speech. We don't mind hearing it twice." He finally agreed.

Clymene, joining in, reminded him, "First, welcome and thank all who have come. Second, express your gratitude for the Olympians and your ancestors. Third, move on to listing your plans and aspirations, and fourth, invite others to join you in achieving them. Finally, close with grateful thanks to your father for all he has done and ask him for a simple gift, like a ring or a garland."

Phaethon bit his lips, collecting his thoughts. Secretly, he still held high hopes that if he asked him publicly, his father would succumb to his wish and agree to let him ride his chariot for a day after all. He started with, "Praise Zeus and all the Olympians who have brought me to live in the House of Helios. Praises be to Helios, my father; Clymene, my mother; Perse, our queen; and my cousins who came to join this celebration." He giggled, amused, and continued after a self-important cough. "My honored father, I have but one wish to ask of you on this auspicious occasion. I only want to have you lend me your chariot for a day so that I can bring daylight to the world tomorrow!"

Clymene cried out, covering her eyes in distress, "Not again! No, you will not, Phaethon."

His cousins joined their aunt in coaxing him: "Don't be arrogant, Phaethon. You will embarrass us. You *will* embarrass yourself!"

He stepped down from the dais maintaining a superior look, ignoring the women. "I don't understand him at all! My father is so stingy," he shouted. He felt offended, willing to challenge Helios. After all, he was his heir! "Don't try to make me change my mind," he declared, and stomped out of the room.

His mother begged him, calling out, "Son, you will only make him angry."

"I don't care. I will ask him again. He *will* change his mind!"

That afternoon, Clymene sought her sister, enveloped in a pelt of fear, dropping in on her unexpectedly. She knew her son's stubborn nature and feared the worst. She found Perse settled in front of a large brass mirror, putting the final touches on her makeup for the night.

"He is stubborn and arrogant, dear Perse, not mature enough, and he is definitely not ready. I fear Helios will disown him," she whimpered once she had described the confrontation with Phaethon, her wide cheekbones wet with tears.

"Disrespectful," Perse agreed. "Would he dare?"

"He has not given up, and I don't trust what he will do. How can I stop him?"

Clymene watched Perse quickly move to her special table, the one covered with small and large containers, her tools for creating perfumes and magic. She studied her collection. Finally, she picked up an empty vial and poured a small amount of the perfume she had prepared for guests. Then she carefully added a few drops of liquid stored in a red container and offered it to her sister. "This would make him act drunk. It would weaken his throat muscles and balance. When he musters the energy to give his speech, he will lose his ability to speak and get wobbly. His own energy will activate these properties. Use it if you think it will help to stop him."

Clymene dried her eyes and looked at her sister, surprised, but took the vial. "It has come to this. Please, don't tell anyone."

Starting down the hallway, troubled, she whispered a half-hearted, "Thank you."

EIGHT

PHAETHON'S PARTY AND GUESTS

*I*n preparation for the celebration, Clymene and her nieces dressed in heavily embroidered robes, adding golden chains around their necks, bracelets, and rings set with rubies and emeralds on their fingers. Before coming down to the Great Hall, they went to the palace temple to invoke Athena's aid. Worried for Phaethon's stubborn demands, Clymene asked the temple priest to pray for a successful evening and protection for Helios's son and to offer a sacrificial lamb to the goddess.

The priest was a student of the high art of predicting the future. In his mauve priestly vestments, he slaughtered the animal, removed the liver and gallbladder, and studied them to deduce the will of the goddess. When he returned from the interior of the temple, he told them, "The signs are not crystal clear, but I believe wise Athena, who abhors battles after the deadly Trojan War and Odysseus's disastrous adventures, is cautioning you to keep Phaethon away from horses."

It was a concerning sign, leaving Clymene to worry aloud, "Why? Has he displeased the Olympians?"

"Perhaps unbeknownst to you," said the priest, "Athena

and Zeus have been watching the boy, because he will soon be of age to serve his father and, it is hoped, eventually assist him."

Lampetia responded to her aunt reassuringly, her golden bracelets jingling loudly as she reached to give her a hug. "Don't worry, dear aunt. Athena doesn't know him yet. He will impress her and the other Olympians tonight."

Clymene could tell, though, that the priest had been hesitant when he delivered his message, as happened from time to time. Omens, after all, could occasionally turn out cloudy and useless.

Even so, she looked forward to the evening's festivities, as Helios's celebrations were known for their exuberance and opulence. No expense was spared, starting with the decorations and continuing in the variety of food and entertainment. Servers crisscrossed the crowd with trays of appetizers, olives, cheese, fresh fruit, and poured wine, keeping cylices filled. Trumpeters sounded their long, bronze salpinges to announce Clymene and her nieces' arrival. Phaethon's mother entered the Great Hall in stately grace, her eyes searching for her son, who was late to his celebration. "Monitor him, girls," she whispered to Phaethusa and Lampetia. The young nymphs with glinting hair and gracious manners were willing.

Clymene moved on to make small talk with palace courtiers, locals, and emissaries, all dressed in their spring finery. It was a feast to see the colorful tunics and jewelry, and listen to conversations in different dialects. Most guests, she was sure, came to pay tribute to Helios's house. The sun-god's influence had increased in the Mediterranean world that depended on him to bring light and heat and to change the seasons. *But they are also curious about Phaethon, and what future his father envisions for him.*

When Clymene caught sight of the emissary from Ethiopia, she sought him out, weaving through the crowd. She recognized him from her years living with Merops, king of Ethiopia, her protector and Phaethon's guardian-father figure in his early childhood. The emissary approached her, resplendent in his ample white cotton, floor-length tunic decorated with a traditional fringe in gold, emerald-green, red, and mauve colors. She smiled, eager to get news from that house.

"I bring you and Phaethon the emperor's greetings and good wishes for good health and fortune, my lady." He raised his hand over his tight, curly hair and headdress decorated with high colorful bird plumes and took a low bow.

Clymene returned a slight bow and answered in dialect, "I am very fond of your country, King Merops, and memories of my days in Ethiopia. I hope he is well. Please, give him regards from me and my son! We are well." She smiled wistfully.

"It has been two years since you left our kingdom, my lady. We all miss you and Phaethon and hope you will visit us again someday. My king is happy to see your improved station in life at Helios's house, one you well deserve."

She considered his words and said, "It is an auspicious day that will mark my son's future." Then she asked the emissary to share news about Merops's private life, carrying out the conversation in whispers so that others would not hear any confidential news. "Tell me who keeps him company?" she asked, leaning closer.

The emissary answered her kindly. "In the past two years, he has had women interested in him but has not chosen another. The king will be pleased to know you look well."

"When did you see him last?" she asked anxiously. "Is he happy?"

"I saw him right before I came to this gathering. He sends you his love and misses you."

Clymene gave him a medallion with raised sunbursts, a souvenir to take to Merops. "Tell him I often think of him and wish him well." The sound of salpinges announcing new arrivals interrupted their conversation.

By the time Phaethon arrived, the Great Hall was brimming with guests from all corners of the Mediterranean, neighboring courts, mortals, nymphs, and demigods. The differing dialects, exotic clothes, and varieties of headwear spoke of a cosmopolitan crowd.

When the salpinges sounded, the crowd turned to greet her son with, "Hail, Phaethon, son of Helios!" In his elegant clothes, adorned with a turquoise stone garland his mother had sent for him, he made a splendid entrance.

Clymene knew that the boy's reputation was not stellar among the palace courtiers, but it did not seem to matter to Phaethon, who moved easily through the crowd, greeting townspeople and travelers, eventually joining Orion and his hunting friends in the garden.

Servers carried trays piled high with fish and meat steaming hot from the kitchens and laid them out on the long table set near the walls of the hall. Guests were milling around, enjoying the food and wine. Clymene watched her son in the garden, laughing and chatting brightly with his young friends, as Lampetia and Phaethusa made their way to meet him. His friends fanned praises on him, and he smiled and bowed. *He is so hungry for approval*, thought Clymene. Around her, she heard the accolades: "He is so handsome," and "His future is bright!"

In his mother's eyes, Phaethon certainly had princely bearings. He was her boy, and she expected to see him someday inspire and lead others—but today she did not trust him. She walked past the pillars to the courtyard, took him by his arm, and handed him a small vial. "You forgot to use your perfume." He took it and discreetly applied some to his arms and wrists, returning the vial to his mother. Then the two moved back in the Great Hall to make the rounds. Softly she whispered, "Be a good host. Remember to have your friends' cylices filled before your own."

The room was getting stiflingly warm, as servants started lighting torches to welcome the evening hours. Musicians played their tunes, singing praises to the Olympian gods. The cithara and the aulos players accompanied a vocalist singing more silvery melodies, extolling the virtues of the sun. When the music stopped, Clymene and all the crowd got quiet and turned to listen to a visiting bard who announced he would entertain them with stories about the aftermath of the Trojan War. Perse had invited him because he did not hesitate to reveal the barbarity of war.

The bard's name was Homer. He was a middle-aged man who had been living in the guest wing of Helios's court for the past three days. He had accepted Perse's invitation when she met him on the island of Chios at "Homer's rock" surrounded by a group of mesmerized students, teaching them to compose in Ionic pentameter. Since his arrival at Helios's palace had coincided with Phaethon's celebration, he came to the gathering to earn his keep entertaining his hosts and their guests. In a simple white tunic, stroking his graying beard, he began performing his rhapsodies for the small crowd that had gathered around him to hear the latest adventures of Odysseus.

An enthusiastic crowd clapped, wanting more, but he took a break from his performance to chat with Helios's guests. With the well-modulated voice of an actor, he answered their questions about the warrior king and his most recent adventures on his journey back home: "No, he has not returned to Ithaca yet, and I think he is still alive. He has been tested by the Olympian gods and has lost some men. Who knows what he endured since he left Skylla's rock?"

The aftermath of the Trojan War was a popular subject in courts. The bard readily recounted Odysseus's harrowing crossing of the Strait of Messina, where he was caught between the monster Skylla and the deadly whirlpool Charybdis and barely survived, but lost six sailors who were devoured by the monster.

Homer continued, "Such a reckless king! Rumor has it that one of his sailors, a troublemaker, was stirring the crew to mutiny against him. The sailors were exhausted from the war and the long journey home."

When the two nymphs, Phaethusa and Lampetia, joined the small crowd that had gathered around him, he introduced them, then said, "After Skylla, I heard the sailors survived another gale and set sails for Trinacia. It's the island where Lady Phaethusa and Lady Lampetia keep Helios's cattle."

"Our home," said Phaethusa, smiling. "Yes, Odysseus is still alive. He warned his crew to keep their hands off all herds at Trinacia, for this has been Helios's sanctuary for his cattle for centuries . . ."

". . . to leave the cattle alone, even if the men run out of food and drink," finished Lampetia, "which they listened to, at first. They fished and caught birds, but then—"

"We were alarmed," Phaethusa interrupted her. "It was one of the troublemakers who roused the sailors to disobey Odysseus and ignore his warnings not to hurt the herd."

Intrigued, Homer raised his bushy eyebrows and, leaning in, asked, "I heard that the king of Ithaca had made his crew take an oath to obey him. He would have ordered them to leave the cattle alone, for he knew great harm would come to them if they did not. Didn't he?"

"Yes, it's true. Circe had warned him. But they did run out of food and drink, and the troublemaker convinced them that dying of hunger was a slow death, worse than the sudden death of an avenging Helios," Lampetia said evenly. "They violated Helios's sanctuary!"

Homer watched Phaethusa wrap her arms around herself, her chin quivering. "I smelled the cattle's burning flesh in the wind; I saw their hides creeping about as if they were alive and heard their mourning cries coming off the spits." Slowly she added, "When Odysseus returned, the carnage horrified him, but it was too late."

Lampetia's voice rang with anger. "I told my father. They had slaughtered and roasted the flesh on spits, the monsters! My father was so angry! He threatened the pantheon of Mount Olympus that he would no longer shine on this earth again."

The small crowd held their breath. The end of the world? It was not the first time a god had threatened the life of mortals. The bard looked at Lampetia and commented calmly, "But the sun still rises and sets."

She finished her story. "Zeus pleaded with our father to keep shining on the earth and promised to avenge the murders. He spread dark clouds over Trinacia and turned on a furious gale that crashed Odysseus's ship, submerging the mast. The waves drowned one man after the other until the only one left was Odysseus, drifting forlorn, perched on a raft."

Homer reached for a cylix and took a long swallow to wet his throat. He was pleased. This updated information, straight from the source, would be the basis of new rhapsodies!

Later that evening, Clymene whispered to the bard, "I don't think Odysseus is a hero. Look what he put his men through for Trojan gold and loot. So many have died. Where are his men and the loot now? Down at the bottom of the sea! What kind of king is he? What will he say to their families in Ithaca?"

The bard smiled and whispered back, "The bloodshed and adventures of Troy are tragic. I wish more gods opposed war, but it makes for a wonderful epic."

61

"My sister aspires to encourage peace. Maybe you will tell stories about that someday."

He took a slight bow, touched his beard thoughtfully, and said, "My heart has learned to glow for others' good and melt at others' woe." Wise as he was, deep down, the famous bard wished his rhapsodies would someday aid Queen Perse.

Soon after, the piercing sound of the salpinges announced Helios and Perse. Back from his daily trek, the sun-god shone, wearing gold chains around his chest, arm bracelets on both arms, and a crown of sunrays on his hair. He wore a crocus-yellow tunic, belted with linked stars, and two rings—one was a plain band, and the other was decorated with raised sunbursts. The queen, who carried herself proudly, wore a thin lime-green tunic that highlighted her curvy lines. Leonora had arranged Perse's long blonde hair to unfold in curly waves. She was wearing her favorite perfume, pearl earrings, and a belt of coiled snake joints wrapped around her trim waist. Exclamations of admiration filled the hall. All those present greeted them with deafening cheers: "Hail to Helios! Hail to Perse! Glory be!"

Helios moved toward his throne, checking the decorations and still admiring his daughter Circe's gift, a tapestry mounted behind the throne, that was coming alive. It was as if spring breezes were dancing through it, swaying the grasses and wildflowers scattered in spring fields, which the sun's magic rays caressed. A smile blossomed on the sun-god's lips when he saw the enameled copper sunbursts covering the ceiling. Perse followed his eyes and whispered, "Clymene has done an extraordinary job. Be sure to praise her."

"I will."

The couple stopped to talk to notable guests, court emissaries, Phaethon's friends, Helios's army guards, and temple priests.

The sun-god and Perse spoke at length with the bare-chested emissary from Crete, whom their daughter Pacifae and King Minos of Crete had sent. He wore gold chains and a decorative apron with tassels around his trim waist. The young man presented Helios with a gold medallion depicting the Cretan king and queen. Helios thanked him and Perse inquired whether the royals were pleased with the labyrinth, work of the Athenian builder Daedalus. The emissary's gaze shifted at once from Perse to the sun-god. *He knows I am being blamed for the death of the boy Icarus,* thought Helios. *Even though it was Minos who imprisoned Daedalus and his son.* Though reddened to the roots of his hair, the emissary praised the project, then bowed slightly and looked away as Perse left her husband's side to join his daughters at the raised stage in the center of the hall.

The all-knowing Helios commented, "I saw new skirmishes breaking out outside Athens and Minos's men fighting against the Athenians. I hope they can soon settle their differences. We don't need another Trojan War." He knew that the king of Crete was ambitious. It was not beyond him to send men to the continent to invade and conquer new lands.

The emissary disclosed, "Athenians killed one of Minos's sons. He had to respond, my lord." They soon lapsed into a discussion about matters of trade and newly formed alliances among Greek city-states.

When Helios finally settled on his throne, servants brought him trays of delectable food. He saw Phaethon, who had parted from the garden with Orion and his mother, move closer to the stage and wave at his father, raising his cylix high in the air. Helios pursed his lips. *The boy has been downing copious quantities of red wine all night.*

When Clymene moved to center stage and took her lyre in her hands, the sun-god got on his feet and placed his index finger on his lips. "Shh . . ." The hall fell quiet as Clymene strummed the strings gently, releasing a soft melody, and settled on the refrain.

"It's the spring of his life.
May all gods grant
Wings to his dreams . . ."

Helios loved listening to her satin voice that stirred potent emotions spilling out from her heart. Helios understood how to find and appreciate talented women to mate with. He knew Clymene loved her son and she hoped he would be the heir of the House of the Sun. As she strummed the final chords, the hall broke into thunderous applause and he joined.

By the time he had to give his speech, Phaethon seemed tipsy, unsteady on his feet. Helios watched him stagger through the crowd with a silly grin on his face. Giggling, he smashed his cylix, pieces scattering hither and yon. People started snickering at his expense. He moved to climb the stage steps, and with Orion's help, he settled on his chair. The sun-god noticed the look of alarm on Orion's face. *He is a true friend*, he thought.

Hopeful that the boy could still manage despite his condition. Helios was about to call for his speech—but Clymene approached the throne and whispered to him, "Please, take charge. Phaethon is drunk. He can't deliver a speech, dear." She pointed to the chair where her son had dropped, still giggling.

Immediately, Helios drew attention to himself. In a stentorian voice, feigning no disturbance at the sight of his son, he asked for a cylix filled with wine and invited the guests: "Raise it to my son. Wish him health, wealth, and protection of the gods. May his days be bright, and may he never cast a shadow!"

The crowd responded, calling out their wishes. Pleased, Helios walked to the stage, saying, "Within the year, Phaethon will be ready to join the palace guard. My family is gifting him the tools a soldier needs to practice battle skills. Today I have a gift for him to wear that signifies he is a prince, my honored son." With that, he took off the ring decorated with sunbursts and showed it to the crowd. An awed hum rose in the room.

The boy could muster only a faint, "Thank you, Father." Helios joined his son on the stage and placed the ring on Phaethon's middle finger.

Perse moved near her nephew, laid her hand on his shoulder, and said, "Here is my gift, dear Phaethon, a gift you can use on the days you practice riding Helios's horses and, someday, his chariot across the sky. May Artemis, Zeus, and Hera protect you!"

The attendant raised each bridle in the air for the crowd to see: gleaming leather and sparkling emeralds. The young people clapped, and whispered oohs and aahs rose from the crowd.

Helios knew that Phaethon was a lost cause and would be unable to thank those showering him with praises and gifts. The family hovered, surrounding him. Helios returned to his throne, remained standing, and spoke to the court. "Thank you for joining my family in celebrating with us Phaethon's passage birthday. It is a memorable night for our family, and we appreciate and especially honor those who traveled to be here." He checked with Clymene, who waved for him to go on. "It has been a long day and morning comes soon, my honored guests. I hope you had a good time, and I bid you goodnight!" He turned to leave, his head held high, but he was overcome by a sinking feeling. He was glad it was over.

The crowd started dispersing, staring at Phaethon, who seemed unable to get on his feet. Clymene asked Perse to give him a whiff of salts, and he came to. Staggering, the boy leaned on Orion and his mother, and they started for his quarters.

Indignant, he slurred these words: "I asked for a gift befitting the son of Helios. What do I get? A ring and four bridles!"

Clymene hushed him and smiled the faintest of smiles. She was fatigued from disappointment, from the long day and the late hour of the night. She softly patted Phaethon's arm. "Your father loves you. He wants to give you the gift, but only when you can safely receive it."

Perse leaned toward her sister and whispered frostily, "I am glad he is your son, Clymene. No disrespect intended, but I worry about how cocky your boy is."

Clymene cringed. She did not need her sister's sarcasm.

It was getting late. Clymene looked up at the stars and thought of Selene, riding her chariot over the night sky, traveling to the cave to meet her shepherd. She thanked Orion for helping her get Phaethon upstairs to his bedroom.

The guests, weary from the long evening and the unexpected turn of events, scattered toward the exits and into the night.

NINE

THE AFTERMATH

Pacing in his chamber, Helios spoke with a raspy voice, "I will not forget the grief, the embarrassment this boy caused me tonight!"

Perse took his hand and gave it a squeeze. "Teens are unpredictable, dear. Remember your youth? The time you and your friends drank mortal beer and staggered home? Your father found you sleeping in the cellar, and he still tells the story! Every youth goes down the same bumpy road. Didn't you?"

She saw Helios purse his lips. "I expected more from a son of mine." He drew his eyebrows together, trying to hide a smile. "Don't excuse him so easily. You women need to stop spoiling him." He started to undress.

What is it about this father and his sons? she wondered, recalling that when their son, Aeetes, refused to obey and join Helios's soldier war games, the sun-god showed no patience. That was when both Circe and Aeetes left the family home.

Perse slipped into his bed, watching him, and spoke in soothing tones. "The boy will grow up. He is not your only child who is going through a rough patch. Aeetes was rebellious." She knew he would remember their own children's sudden departure, seeking independence, a path of their own.

She also knew that to Helios, it was an old story best forgotten.

"The boy's behavior angers me because he is not an uncouth barbarian. How could he lose his senses on the evening of his special celebration? I should keep him confined for a few days to realize what a sorry embarrassment he is to this family."

Though Perse's voice was calm, her message was pointed. "Sometimes you are simply adamant that Phaethon is nothing but trouble! Have faith in time. Don't jinx him to the Olympians. He needs your protection and theirs. Every child does," she persisted, raising her eyebrows.

Helios's face turned red.

Is he taking my words as provocation, she wondered, *or might he actually be listening?*

He kicked off his sandals, then snapped off his belt and dropped it to the floor. He walked to the window, his nostrils flaring, anger bubbling up under the surface, and turned back suddenly. "He came to this place seeking to meet me, his father," Helios spat. "I welcomed him, wanted to be proud of a son that grew up like a tree, leafing strong, but tonight somebody—he himself or perhaps a god—shook his good senses."

"One must honor their blood. He is your son. Clymene is a wonderful mother. In time, you will give him a home and land, and a wife to raise a family. Give him a chance. Deep down he admires you. He is your noble son. Asim will help him settle down. Let's get some sleep." Tired of coaxing him, she invited him to their bed. When he came, Perse tussled his hair.

"I am worn out," he said as he lay down, pulling the covers over them both.

The next morning, Clymene went to her desk and tried to write some new lines about the night before. Phaethon's public drunken behavior had darkened her mood. He would be the talk of the town for days to come. Her pen would drop only dark ink, mournful thoughts. It could have been worse, but could she ever regain her footing and optimism about the future? Her boy had not been an easy son to raise. Was that her fault?

The queen's sister moved to the next room and settled on spinning thread all morning. No weaving. Rhythmically twirling the spinner with her practiced fingers was soothing. When Melpomene came in to tidy up, she scolded her for not bringing her a snack and sent her away. The evening had left her wondering if their sacrifice of leaving Merops for the shiny palace of Helios had been worthwhile. The comforts of palatial living had done little for her son. As for herself, she did not need all the fuss and luxury. The long thread she was spinning led her to the bottom of the well of despair she had tried to avoid. Her hopes for Phaethon's future had sunk last night. *Helios must be angry.*

When Perse came to see her, Clymene, with an edge to her voice, ordered Melpomene, who was always hovering within earshot: "Bring more wool. And ask my nieces to join me."

She did not need more wool, but she needed to get rid of her maid, who was becoming a witness to her distress.

Melpomene moved away into the palace shadows without a word.

The sisters stayed quiet for a while, and then Clymene sat up straight. "You know," she said, "his anger may be short-lived, but Phaethon's drinking and his strange obsession with Helios's horses bode trouble. We were happier when we lived in Ethiopia, before he learned Helios was his father."

Perse patted her back. "Sister, let Melpomene take care of you. Take a bath, visit with our nieces. Time will take care of us, and last night will be forgotten."

"I doubt if my son met with Asim this morning—I should check on him."

"It may be best to let them work things out, Clymene."

"I will ask my nieces to remind him," she said, disheartened.

Over the next few days, the queen noticed that her sister was overcome with grief about Phaethon's miserable behavior. Her words were few and her coloring pale, her eyes had dark circles around them, and her appetite was gone. She had been avoiding public appearances. The few times she came to the Great Hall, she was bent like a weeping willow. Perse meant to help her sister regain confidence and courage.

One afternoon, the queen invited Phaethusa, Lampetia, and Clymene to join her in her gazebo, under the wisteria. There was a pleasant breeze out when they arrived and Leonora, along with her helpers, carried drinks, fruit, and honey to the table. The conversation drifted to reminiscences.

"Remember our growing-up years, in our parents' care, Clymene?" the queen mused when they had all settled around the table.

"Those were innocent years," Clymene agreed with a tired smile.

"Then we saw Zeus and his gang of bloodthirsty gods tilt the world off-balance with wars and competitions," said Perse, raising her voice.

She looked at her nieces, wondering how they felt about humanity's troubles. "Our mother, Tethys, filled my heart with lofty aspirations then," she continued. "I still carry them. Surrounded by powerful allies, our parents ruled the waters. They loved the earth and mortals."

"You were always more ambitious than I," Clymene acknowledged.

A new thought sprang to Perse's mind. This was an opportunity to initiate her nieces to her secret plan to develop a women's alliance of goddesses, something she had been envisioning for some time. She had talked about this dream with Clymene, who told her that she thought this too lofty. Perse sometimes felt that her sister humored her but expected nothing to come of her ideas. Turning to Phaethusa and Lampetia, she asked, "What has your mother told you about your grandmother Tethys?"

"Not much," both women responded in unison.

"Ah, there is more to share then!"

"Some say that Tethys and Oceanus were the parents of creation." Phaethusa became bolder, surprising her aunt. "Recently, Grandmother Tethys has been staying all on her own, apart from her husband. They say she still exudes confidence and majesty."

"As fond as I am of Mother," Clymene answered, "I can't see why she lives by herself, rebelling against Oceanus. What could she possibly gain from that?"

"They say she left him to stop the floods that were endangering mortals," Lampetia cut in.

Perse bristled. "Nonsense!" She turned to Clymene. "It's not anarchy, dear. It's claiming her place and ours in the world! Grandfather is an autocrat. Mother seeks her own kinder, softer world. Look at the death and devastation in Troy, just to entertain the Olympians! Who is the victor? The Greeks have left so many dead behind! Mother was against this war. There had to be other ways to keep the peace."

The queen felt herself grow animated. "Boys and men take a lot of space and need us to balance them to succeed," she continued, her voice escalating, "but we can also set our own direction and create. We need more space than we are granted!" She was watching her nieces and saw that Lampetia was smiling. "What do you think?"

"I am certain that you and Grandmother Tethys are right!"

Perse nodded, feeling satisfaction. She could count on Phaethusa too. Those two walked their lives in lockstep. "Other Olympian goddesses see it my way. I know that wise old Cybele does—so do Hera and Demeter."

Perse, energized, spoke from her heart and her nieces listened. "That is how I have faith that we can help each other and rise above Zeus's patriarchal hegemony. We can help Selene. Mother taught us about the richness and power of women. She talked about women who wrote poetry, created music, and partook in philosophical discussions. They also led cities. I know they fought, ruled over armies, hunted like men. I don't choose that way of life, but we are equally strong as men."

"You do sound like our mother," said Clymene, sounding exasperated.

"There are stories of the matriarchs we have unearthed to understand our past. Even Cerveros, who guards the entrance to the land of the dead, cannot undercut us in life. The blood that runs in our veins comes from royal stock. We need a core of us to form a council that would intervene and negotiate with Zeus and his followers."

Perse realized Clymene was concerned, but her nieces were seeing her vision of a new world; there was a dreamy quality and hope in their eyes.

"They will not let you, dear Perse!" Clymene warned.

"I am starting small, with a Great Hall for our gatherings, sister," the queen answered. "Even before that, we can start working together. We can solve smaller issues, like Selene's troubles!"

"Oh, dear!" Clymene muttered.

Perse glared at her sister and said, "Someday, I hope an older Phaethon will join us in that work. Peace needs many allies."

TEN

BEGINNINGS

A sim, the wise Egyptian teacher, waited for Phaethon at the stables. Looking to the sky, he saw that Eos was nearly ready to hand off the day. *But likely Helios has not yet risen from his bed to head to the stables,* he mused.

The stable master was wary about giving lessons to Phaethon, whose reputation for insolence and impatience preceded him, but it was Helios's order. Asim was a tall man. His olive skin was a mark of his proud heritage, and he was a patient man. He came from the holy Egyptian city of Memphis, where his father kept a traveler's hotel, a well-known caravanserai, as the people called it, with stables for horses and camels to rest for a day and rooms for the desert nomads to stay for a night. He had been with the sun-god ever since he was a young man, loyal, knowledgeable, and devoted to Helios.

This morning, after the sun-god's departure, Asim had a couple of stable hands clean the outdoor arena and line the tack he would introduce to Phaethon. He had brought a handful of carrots for a friendly introduction to Blaze, the easygoing gelding that was eating barley in his paddock.

A glance at the progress of the sun in the sky told him that Helios's son was late leaving the palace of one thousand rooms.

Asim, whose name means "protector," paced between the pad-dock and the arena, thinking about the lesson and his student, who had quite an ending to his celebration. A server had told the stable hands the boy was so drunk, his friend Orion, Clymene, and an attendant had to carry him to his bed. *Best to start slowly,* he thought: introduce Phaethon on how to care for his horse before showing him how to ride him and perhaps let him mount the horse for a quick ride. In his forties, Asim had a reputation in town for being a student of the healing medicines, treating horses and ailing palace dogs. His manner was soft and calm, and his knowledge, experience, and willingness to help were well-known.

When Phaethon and his cousins arrived, Asim was brush-ing the horse. The youth approached him, running. "I am ready, master, for my lesson." Blaze shied away.

The teacher took a quick bow, greeting Lampetia and Pha-ethusa, who immediately returned to the palace. He set the brush by the fence. "Come and meet Blaze, Master Phaethon," he said, and, taking the reins, walked the horse to the arena. He gave Phaethon some carrots for the horse and watched Blaze stop gnawing at the bit and turn toward the hand that held the treats. "He is a sweet gelding. You will get to know each other well. He loves carrots. Have you been around horses before?"

The young equestrian's lower lip protruded in a pout as he took the carrots. "I have seen my father riding his in the sky some mornings. It is what I want to do too, but he won't let me."

Asim pressed his lips together in a slight grimace. "Your father is a master horseman, and you will be one too. There is a lot to learn. Be patient and calm around your horse. These animals can readily pick up tension, and it makes it harder to work with them."

Phaethon lowered his eyes, saying, "Tell me what I need to do. I will practice until I know how." He held out the carrots for Blaze, who lifted them in his mouth with his tongue.

Asim watched a broad smile light up his student's face. It was a good start. "When you arrived, I was brushing him. It's a good way for the horse to get to know you, so that's how we will start." The stable master picked up the brush and demonstrated. "When you are grooming him, face the opposite direction to your horse's head, working on his side. Use a circular motion with the brush if you are removing dried mud. Here."

"The grooms can do that for me," answered Phaethon abruptly. "I just want to learn how to ride."

The teacher kept holding out the brush. "Horses are large, powerful animals. You want them to be your partners. It's best to be their friend. They will remember your touch and smell, and get to recognize you this way. Come, Phaethon, try it. Blaze will love it just as he loved taking carrots from your hands."

"Well, just for a few strokes, then. But I just want to ride him."

"You want to ride a friend? Feel the hair. Brush his body to clear the mud. He loves to roll on the ground, and he loves to be brushed. I have already worked on his belly and legs. You can finish brushing his back. See? He is waiting, still." Asim took a step back, and the boy took the brush.

The stable master watched Phaethon for a while and then brought the bridle Helios and Perse had gifted him and mounted it on the horse, making final adjustments. Then he took the lunge line and attached it to the bit.

"The next thing we do is walk Blaze around the arena. It helps him loosen his joints and get some exercise. Do you want to hold the line? I will watch you from this corner."

Asim stood on the sidelines, ready to intervene, but Phaethon fell into a smooth rhythm, walking beside the horse a few rounds along the edge of the arena. Then he called out to Asim, "When will I ride him, master?"

"He is ready now. Move to the middle of the arena and let a good length of his lunge line out. He knows this routine. He will walk, then trot, then canter around. Just hold on to the line and watch him let out some pent-up energy."

Phaethon followed instructions and watched the horse speed up and eventually slow down. After a while, he asked again, "When can I ride him, master?"

"You will, soon. You will get used to bareback riding, Phaethon. We will end your first lesson with a brief ride. I will help you mount Blaze, and you can get a feel of being on a horse," Asim said reassuringly.

"I am ready today; you are so slow. This will take forever," Phaethon complained, approaching the horse. Still holding the line, he took an impertinent leap, not high enough to mount Blaze, and fell to the ground.

Asim, surprised and quick as the wind, ran to help the boy get up, taking the rope and calming the horse. "Are you hurt?"

Phaethon seemed dazed. "No, no! I am fine," he said.

Asim lent him a hand to get up and motioned for him to step to the side. The horse kicked his front hooves impatiently. "Your father asked me to teach you well and keep you safe. Tomorrow we will use a cloth on Blaze's back. For now, watch me." He took a pad that was on the fence and described his actions as he was taking them. "I just laid the pad on his back. Holding the reins, I am taking hold of the withers along his mane, and then I slip my leg over his bare back."

"Asim, I can do that now!" Phaethon walked to the fence, his face still red, his tunic dusty. But Asim was already on Blaze.

"Perhaps you can, but we will practice mounting him the right way tomorrow. See how I am standing proud, my legs astride, pressing his sides? He is ready to go to a canter. More practice tomorrow." Asim dismounted and called a groom to bring a bucket of barley and hand it to Phaethon.

"Shake it," he said.

Blaze's ears perked up, and he came to Phaethon slowly, snorting.

"Soon, we will ride the trails that run up through the woods and down to the shoreline. More to come, my boy," Asim said, then watched a hopeful smile form on Phaethon's face.

The horse pawed his feeding bucket.

Marble, metal, rock, and wood. An understanding of many materials, their strength, the aesthetic of textures, and his ability to plan and coordinate with people involved in his projects were some of what elevated Athenian Daedalus into fame. Word had spread in the Mediterranean world about his creation, the miraculous architectural wonder of the palace of Knossos on the island of Crete, and Perse was well aware of him. King Minos, a mighty ruler, and his wife, Pacifae, Perse's daughter, held their councils and kept their family riches and secrets inside its walls. For those in the know, there were intrigues in and out of the bedrooms, lush supplies in storage, and a labyrinth where a mysterious creature was kept under lock and key. The Minotaur was the product of Pacifae's lust; she had fallen in love with a bull and birthed the beast, much to Minos's embarrassment.

Though the royals of Crete praised the famous designer of the Minoan architectural wonder, they also imprisoned him and his son, Icarus, on their island to keep him to their service. A careful and quiet man, Daedalus built wings for himself and his son. By now, the world knew that father and son had escaped, but the boy's wings, made of beeswax and feathers, melted when he flew high, near the sun, disobeying his father's warnings. Daedalus had buried his son—who'd drowned in the sea—and was grieving, alone and forlorn on the island of Icaria.

Perse could not stop thinking about Daedalus. Now that she felt confident that her efforts to help Selene would succeed, she shared with Clymene her wish to invite Daedalus and entrust him with building the new hall.

The sisters sat at the gazebo drinking fruit juice Leonora had freshly squeezed for them that morning. "Pacifae and Minos have been wretched to this man, don't you think?" Perse demanded of Clymene. "I let my daughter know what I thought. But who better than Daedalus to take charge of the new hall?"

Clymene set her cup down, and Perse felt her sister's disapproving eyes rest on her. "Isn't it premature to bring a builder? Helios has not agreed to this project unless Selene's troubles are over." Her piercing eyes were not letting Perse off the hook.

Undaunted, the queen replied, "You know how these transactions take time to firm up. It is not too early to begin. I don't want to waste time."

"But . . ."

Perse tapped the tabletop lightly, cutting in with, "I am so close now. It will not hurt to invite him and find out if he is willing to take it on."

"In that regard, it is a brilliant idea. He is the best choice, and he would benefit from taking on a new project before he loses his mind from grief. But you are taking a risk. You might anger Helios if he knew. Take your time, dear Perse."

The queen's eyes narrowed as she looked at Clymene. "How would he know, unless you tell him, my sister?"

"Perse, sometimes I wonder if you trust me—or anyone for that matter," she groaned.

Time brought release from dark fears and hope for renewed possibilities for Clymene, who had to move on, although the nagging oracle would rear its ugly head yet again. Her sister's enthusiasm about building a Great Hall and her passion for peace were captivating. She kept up with her progress while watching her son's growing stormy passion for horses. He spent most of his days seeking to learn more skills, and he kept talking to his mother about Helios's team of horses. She was dismayed that he remained awed by the feisty foursome, though her response never disappointed him.

"No rush to ride them," she would answer each time. "They are wild."

Often Clymene would open her windows and doors wide and tune into snorts, neighs, and other sounds coming from the stables. She homed in, listening for Blaze's canter, Phaethon's commands, and Helios's departures and arrivals. From her window, she tracked Blaze and her son riding down to the beach and the small villages around the palace.

The last time she had gone to the stables, the stable master ran into her in the tack room. "Looking for Phaethon? He is making good progress, my lady. This way," he'd said, leading her to the paddock.

She'd tapped his arm twice. "He has a good teacher."

The two had watched then as Phaethon groomed Blaze, while Asim, who had trained the horse himself, explained, "He has fed and watered him already."

Clymene had covered her nose with her handkerchief. "I'll just wait and watch from here." She'd stopped mid-step to avoid a muddy puddle, while he'd bowed, excusing himself and wishing her a good day.

After that, his mother watched Phaethon tend to his horse silently. Blaze was an older, and still fine, chiseled horse that Helios had chosen for his son because of his mellow nature. The horse twitched and quivered as Phaethon rubbed him down with round strokes. Their bond was obvious. Boy and animal were in deep appreciation of each other. For a while, she stood pondering the change in her son. Who knew this could really happen! "Phaethon, are you taking him for a run?" she called out.

He turned, his eyes smiling when he saw her. "We'll be riding to the port, to see what ships have arrived and what goods they bring, Mother. Orion is supposed to meet us there."

"Invite him to stop by the palace afterward." She made him promise. Orion, after all, was a good influence.

Phaethon put the bridle Perse had gifted him on the horse. He took his time. Then taking the reins, he led him to the arena.

"Gorgeous! I am proud of you, son!" she said. "Blaze looks his finest today. I will leave you to your day."

On her way to the Great Hall, Clymene contemplated how her life had fallen into a tranquil path once more. She still thought of Merops fondly and was glad that Helios's attentions were on her sister. He had been so demanding of her time when Perse was away. Now her sister was keeping the sun-god occupied, and her son seemed happy and settled. That freed her to return to her music and poems.

She roamed through the hallways and eventually returned to her quarters, cleaned up, changed her sandals, and joined her sister, who was talking to a couple of palace guards in the Great Hall.

Perse saluted her. "Coming back from the stables? How is Phaethon doing?"

"Well," Clymene said, smiling. "I used to worry about him hurting himself, falling, but he has turned out to be a good rider. He would win any competition with youth his age." She raised her arm high, her bracelets jingling proud.

Perse replied, "I am glad. How lovely that he enjoys his new hobby—and Helios is pleased."

The only cloud that hung over Clymene was the warning she and her nieces had received from the temple on Phaethon's birthday celebration. His mother wished she could dismiss the worry as a mix-up. After all, Asim had praised the boy for his dedication, the hours and care he shared with his fine gelding.

She had sensed a positive shift in her son. He seemed more respectful, responsible, and willing to listen to her advice.

ELEVEN

A PLAN
FOR SELENE

L ife returned to its old familiar pitter-patter at Hyperion Helios's palace, and it was time for Perse to focus on ways to resolve Selene's difficulties. Besides, her husband was getting impatient with her. He complained about the danger of losing his valuable relationship with Zeus, the father of all. "This is still unresolved!" he had grumbled just the day before. "Don't expect a Great Hall of your own."

At least Helios had stopped threatening to harm the shepherd himself, the mortal Selene had taken as her lover. It had been a while since he'd uttered, "It would be so easy to burn him to a crisp. Selene is playing with fire!" It was an idle threat.

The queen resumed her contacts with allies, building on the plan. When the faint light of dawn broke the dark of night, alone in her quarters Perse lifted the mirror and called out, "Eos, have you shared your excellent idea with Selene and Helios?" She repeated the question when she summoned her husband's sister directly and earnestly.

Eos's pale face came into view, and Perse noticed a frown on her face. With a pinched, unhappy expression, she looked into

Perse's eyes. "Zeus does not like meddling women but does not really want to hurt Selene. So, my brother raised it with him, but the Olympian father of all is hesitant. We need more allies to convince him."

"But he did not object! I wonder if Selene would?" Perse smiled to herself, knowing that her special perfume would contribute to their success. Her sister-in-law would soon lose interest in her erotic entanglement with Endymion.

Eos's response was encouraging. "Helios was enthusiastic and hopeful, dear Perse, until he saw Zeus's reaction. Selene really has no choice."

That is when the queen disclosed the secret properties of the perfume destined for Selene, and the two giggled conspiratorially.

"I will appeal to Hera and ask for her support. She might help resolve this impasse with Zeus," concluded Perse. "I think that your solution is brilliant!" And just as she had praised her husband's sister, the mirror dimmed, and their session ended.

Perse planned to meet with Hera but not before settling where to rest Endymion. She knew that Zeus's wife would want a fully-fledged plan before agreeing to advocate for it to her husband. Now it was time to get her nieces involved. She had heard them talk about the cold winter months, Helios's cattle, and the shepherds' wintering island caves. She would fetch the two sisters for a late-night gathering. Allowing them to witness an exchange with Hecate would bring them in quickly and help her gain their support. They were such agreeable girls.

Time grew precious. Before dawn that day, the sisters, Phaethusa and Lampetia, visited the temple to offer libations of wine to Zeus. They harmonized, singing hymns at the altar, praising his might, and asking for his protection for their upcoming journey home. As the golden rays of morning light lifted the darkness around the temple, they started for their rooms to pack for the journey home.

Perse had invited them to the garden after their visit to the temple and complimented them: "Helios is very pleased about how aptly you care for his cattle and honor him, his light, and majesty."

Phaethusa responded with a broad smile. "It's our privilege."

The queen invited them to her quarters for "a very special goodbye night" without disclosing her agenda. "Come and meet mighty Hecate! Have you met her before? She responds when I call for her over my scrying mirror," she said.

"I have never partaken in a scrying mirror session!" exclaimed Lampetia without hesitation.

"It would be special to meet powerful Hecate," added Phaethusa, fixing a clump of wisteria flowers in her hair. "We need to finish packing."

Perse delivered a quick goodbye. "I will send Leonora to fetch you later tonight."

At the appointed hour, intrigued by the unexpected invitation, the sisters followed Leonora, journeying through the marble corridors and through the Great Hall to the quiet garden. It was a mild night. An owl hooted as a mild breeze swept through the garden. They settled near the fountain to wait for the queen.

Perse walked out, showered by the full moon's silver rays softening the darkness. She prominently carried her scrying mirror, cradling it in her hands, and welcomed the sisters. Their eyes were fixed on the elegant obsidian with the still snake head, visible under Perse's manicured fingers.

"Eerie," Lampetia whispered.

Perse wasted no time, setting the mirror down on the table and explaining, "Hecate, the mighty sorceress, will meet us here tonight. Remember Selene's predicament with her shepherd lover? We are looking for a way to save her from Zeus's wrath. Tonight I hope that with Hecate's wisdom, we will resolve Selene's troubles. We all desire to lend a hand to keep her safe." The sisters felt their aunt's eyes rest on them expectantly.

"You honor us," Lampetia spoke without hesitation, "summoning us to witness your meeting with Hecate. Let us know how we can help our father's sister."

"Thank you for including us," added Phaethusa.

"Shall we move behind you, to watch?" asked Lampetia.

Perse remained standing. "Yes. I will turn my mirror so you can view Hecate when she arrives."

With that, the sisters watched the queen shut her eyes and appear to relax. In the silence that followed, Lampetia held Phaethusa's hand and squeezed it in anticipation. When their aunt opened her eyes, it seemed that Perse's face reflected an inner glow. The sisters sensed the aura of the dark queen's presence. They heard Hecate's otherworldly voice. "Is that you, Perse, daughter of Tethys?"

"Hecate, protector of our household, I implore you. We call for your help."

When the sorceress spoke again, echoes of her voice returned to Lampetia's and Phaethusa's ears. "Eos told me her plan." The sisters watched Perse turn the mirror in their direction and saw Hecate's dark eyes peering out into the night, but the sorceress paid them no heed.

"Helios carried my special perfume to Selene."

"You are so clever, Perse!" chortled Hecate. "Brilliant! It will be easier if Selene loses interest in her mortal lover. In fact, she might eventually feel relief to be rid of him when Zeus agrees to place him in eternal sleep."

For a moment, Hecate's multiple faces were fully visible. Lampetia held her breath and watched a triple image reflecting light from multiple torches; their rays gave a cool, silvery sheen to the sorceress's skin, hair, and eyes. Phaethusa rose in awe. The sisters both wondered what Perse expected of them.

They felt Hecate looking at them and saw her acknowledge them with a nod. They bowed their heads to show respect. The sorceress smiled and quizzed all three women. "But where will he spend his sleeping days?"

"We have a plan," answered Perse. "Leave that part to me and my nieces. We will shelter him in a cave on their island!"

Phaethusa and Lampetia looked at each other, puzzled, and then at Perse's smiling face, and remained silent. They were awestruck by Hecate and were slowly realizing the reason for Perse's invitation.

Just as quickly as she had appeared, Hecate looked away and whispered her parting words, "I leave it up to you three to arrange!"

The women stood still for a few seconds. Then Phaethusa touched her aunt's shoulder and begged, "May I touch your mirror, Aunt Perse?"

"It knows only my touch, dear. Now that Hecate has met you, perhaps you can seek her on your own; sacrifice to Hecate. She favors us, for we are descendants of Oceanus and Tethys."

"So, all you need is a place to lay the shepherd?" asked Lampetia.

Perse responded immediately with a question. "Your island has many caves. Couldn't Endymion rest in one of them?"

"Of course, if Helios does not mind," said Phaethusa, once she saw her sister nod her agreement.

The queen returned an assuring smile. "He will not mind."

Before departing, Lampetia asked, "Tell us about Selene and the perfume?"

"It stays our secret." Perse winked, with a cunning smile. "Right?"

"Of course," both sisters answered.

"The fragrance is alluring, delicious, pleasing. And it blocks every erotic impulse; there is no arousal for the couple that uses it." All three broke out in amused laughter, admiring the powers and cleverness of the queen.

Their part in the plan had surprised them, but the nieces did not feel coerced. The queen was worthy of their admiration. Their part of the plan was so easy to deliver.

TWELVE

PHAETHON'S DEMISE

Melpomene excused herself to wash up in the kitchen, for her hands were sticky from peeling figs for her mistress. She complained to the other help about Clymene: "She is out of sorts, demanding, changes her mind about everything! 'Bring me this set of earrings—oh no, best to wear Circe's gift. How about some fruit? You brought figs? Too sweet—take them back.'"

One cook stopped stirring the cauldron and glared at her. "You have a simple job, spending your day with your lady, fetching, not like us that labor over a searing fire all day long."

An old hand interrupted them. "She must be restless. It will pass. She is easygoing most of the time."

When Melpomene returned to check on her mistress, she found her doubled up, complaining of a headache. Clymene accused her of being absent too long and preparing bathwater that was too hot.

Exasperated, Melpomene suggested, "Shall we call the temple doctor, my mistress?" as she had run out of ideas.

Finally, Clymene confessed to her that she had stayed awake most of the night before with an unexplained sense of foreboding. "But it must be the cries of seagulls and crows that circled over the palace all afternoon."

Later that day, Clymene left her quarters to visit the temple and made an offering of frankincense with a pleasing fragrance known to be favored by Zeus. She appealed for divine protection over Helios's household, praying for good spirits and good health, but deep down she worried because Phaethon had been avoiding her.

Looking for acceptance of her request, she and the temple priest observed the smoke swirling directly to heaven, leaving them wondering if they had been heard.

As the sun rose above the Aegean Sea the next day, the father of gods and men surveyed his domain, satisfied. He stroked his beard thoughtfully. He liked the quiet of the morning hours, the predictable swelling of light expected of Helios daily. He had noticed Helios's consort's modest offering and ignored it. The queenly Hera and the sparkling-eyed Athena kept him company, preoccupied with a discussion about Athenian alliances. Poseidon was dozing off in his chair.

It was then that Zeus noticed the sun-god's chariot taking a low dip to the land. "Careful!" he shouted, and his cry reverberated across the land. An erratic trek would pose danger. For a moment, the chariot seemed steady, as Aethon, Eous, Phlegon, and Pyrois galloped, regaining their composure. Zeus could see the rider's swirling switch, threatening to whip them, and was thankful when the rider did not. That was not like Helios.

He kept watch, and when all seemed to return to normal, he sat on his throne. But then once again the early sun tumbled in strange, uneven patterns, sometimes distant and dim and other times close and hot as he was dropping lower. Zeus got up from his throne, shaded his eyes and scowled, straining to see the sun-god's chariot swerve wildly. It was changing altitude abruptly, and the rider was unsteady, having trouble balancing and keeping hold of the reins. What was the matter with Helios? He always commanded his horses well. Was he drunk? It was not his usual smooth trek. Zeus worried that the earth could not tolerate the extremes of distance and chill from the life-giving sun, followed by searing closeness to its surface.

"Father, look!" Athena called, pointing south.

In the distance, he could see that the sun-god had been starting fires that had burned the tops of trees on a remote Aegean island; a huge glow of heat and smoke billowed toward the sky. Zeus felt his anger surge. "What is the matter with him?" He called out to his eagles, "Scout near the chariot, make sure Helios is awake, and report back!"

The chariot changed its course, seeming to head toward Mount Olympus.

Athena raised her shield to deflect the sun from her eyes. "Danger! Fires can spread fast," she said somberly.

"He has to stop it," answered Zeus. They watched and waited for the scouting birds.

One eagle returned and perched on the armrest of Zeus's throne. He fluffed his wings and reported, "The rider is not Helios. It is his young son, Phaethon, riding the chariot in the sky."

Zeus squinted to get a better view of the boy. "He looks to be very young."

More fires appeared on the mainland. Zeus winced; he had heard about this young man, and it was not all that good—though perhaps it was even worse than he'd thought.

"He is not as steady as his father. You know, those are not easy horses to manage," said Zeus, worried.

"The boy is trouble," Athena warned. "Where is Helios?"

"Do you see him?" he asked, checking the horizon line. "I don't. I wonder why the sun is rising earlier than usual."

Phaethon was certain he could ride his father's famous horses. If he had any fears, they had dissipated like fog in the sun! The earlier he got to the stables, the easier it would be to take charge. Recently, he had had people bow and scrape in his wake, show respect, accept his demands as orders at the stables—by all but Asim, his teacher. He had slipped out of bed silently, ready to execute his fateful plan, and arrived an hour ahead of Helios. Initially, at least, it had worked. He carried and swung his sword wildly, emboldened by the stable staff's salutation, "Our prince!"

Apparently, no one thought to call Asim.

Ordering a couple of grooms, under the pain of death, to get the chariot ready, he quickly took a whip from the tack room and then he saw Perse's Athenian bridles hanging on the wall, their precious stones glimmering. *Wouldn't it be glorious to use them on my first ride over the earth!* The grooms called for extra help and fitted the bridles on each horse. Once ready, grooms hitched the chariot to the team and Phaethon mounted, rushing everyone with, "Out of my way!" He led the team to the launch. The four horses knew what to do. Snorting with excitement, they took off, their hooves leaving clouds of dust behind. It was as if they did not realize they carried a new rider.

Feeling the momentum of his team, Phaethon let his chest swell with pride. He had succeeded and got away with his father's chariot! He would show them all he was the worthy son of Helios. Even though he was disobeying his father, he hoped to make him proud. The chariot swerved; it was exciting! His hair flew back, whipping to the side, and his knuckles turned white as he gripped the reins, sensing the thrust of the horses' gallop. He turned the whip over the horses' heads.

For a moment he looked up, beyond the clouds. A sense of awe overcame him. What a privilege to ride near worlds unseen, beyond what he knew! The notion of extended life, a universe of stars, a sense of the unknown universe—all of it came as a new perception and resonated inside him. No wonder his father commanded so much respect and admiration from mortals and immortals. He wanted that for himself, that and more, for after all, he, Phaethon, was the natural successor.

But Phaethon's pride would fade quickly.

When he looked ahead, the earth was coming closer and then, switching, he felt rocketed into high altitudes. He tightened his hold on the reins, but the horses no longer minded him, even though he cracked his whip to get their attention. His team was emerging from the clouds, their nostrils wide, their snorts loud, their manes blowing straight back from the force of the wind.

With all coordination falling apart, he feared he might fall off the mutinous chariot, plunge into the abyss, and crack like a watermelon spilling into a thousand pieces. And then came the moment when he saw the bridles on the leading horses come off. The reins got tangled on the horses' hooves, stretched beyond endurance, and snapped. With all guidance lost, the horses sped up helter-skelter.

He screamed at the top of his lungs, "Aethon and Eous . . ." He looked below and saw the glow of flames licking treetops, their branches crackling. Phaethon finished beseeching his team, "Phlegon and Pyrois . . . Slow . . . No . . . No . . ."

Maybe Father Helios will come to the rescue!

But there was no time left for him to panic.

Zeus burned with anger. He scanned every direction, though there was no sign of Helios anywhere. He watched the sun-god's flaming wheels churning faster and faster, setting a course vertically to Gaea, as if intending to drill into the ground.

"Brother, what is he doing?" cried Poseidon, awake and as tense as the others. "If the sea heats up, all water creatures will die!"

Poseidon was not exaggerating. Was it time to decide the life or death of this foolish youth? He did not relish handing out sentences, but Zeus had to intervene. He bristled. By the time he raised his hand, the chariot was listing to the left, a sword was swinging wildly in the air, and Phaethon's whip was dropping to the ground. He saw Athena bite down on her bottom lip. *Does she feel sorry for the boy?*

"Father, it isn't safe," she insisted.

Not sorrow then, he thought. *It must be dread.*

In seconds, he had to weigh his choices: to see heaven and earth destroyed or stop this reckless boy. There was no time to spare, no margins left to send someone else—perhaps Charon—to do the dirty deed. He had to blow him to bits. It would compromise his alliance with Hyperion Helios, a Titan with mighty heritage, but there was no good alternative; there was no question. He would not sacrifice the earth.

He stood up, his arm outstretched, and he hurled not one but three bolts of lightning in succession aimed at the bridles and reins. Deafening, crushing sounds split the air, and the repeat thunder engulfed the universe. He had held Phaethon's gaze, watched the boy's arms flailing in the air, before the lightning struck. A second later, explosive thunder and quaking soil sent Phaethon, the horses, and the chariot hither and yon. Smithereens of dust and annihilation followed the pitiless crush clouding the sky. Instantly, a stench of flesh and blood permeated the air. Helios's son and his prized horses had no chance to scream, whinny, or beg for mercy. Even Poseidon reacted to the ferocity of his brother's actions, cheering, "Hail, Zeus! Just in time."

The father of all heard Hera's commanding call. When he turned, she was pointing to fires that appeared and sparkled on the earth. "Water . . . water . . ." she repeated. "Turn him into water, husband! After all, he is the son of an Oceanid nymph."

Zeus considered his wife with admiration. *Practical, collected, my royal wife.* Although it would bring little consolation to Phaethon's parents, it was a good direction to take in the frenzied moment, meeting the crisis. He wanted to maintain his alliance with Helios. His companion was smart.

The Olympians surrounded him, watching with him the pyre in the sky approach the earth, which was being painted in patches of crimson.

Only Hera had thought of the boy, Phaethon, and Zeus knew why. He was a baby whose birth she had tended, visiting Clymene in the distant reaches of Ethiopia, just as she had done for Perse before her.

He raised both hands and commanded the debris to turn into watery, liquid drops. Then he turned to his wife. "You are a goddess with heart and wisdom."

"The boy perished!" she cried. But her cry was lost among the cheers and praises of Zeus. He had saved the earth from the impending danger. It would have been an explosion, a second coming that would have blasted the hospitable planet out of existence, leaving the Olympian gods homeless.

"Wise Father, you saved our home, the earth, and heaven from burning to a crisp," said Athena.

The turbulence on Mount Olympus was settling and so were the fires, the stench of burning leaves on land. Nothing of substance remained from Helios's son, his chariot, or the horses. Cascading toward the land, unrecognizable particles were falling, some light like snowflakes, others scorched, and still others transparent and heavy with liquid heft. While smoke was rising from the seared earth, Zeus's command, like magic, caused the drops to coalesce with particle vapors and solidify into beads of water, forming rivers, brooks, rivulets, and small lakes that quenched the parched earth. Cosmic dust and water!

Most mortals were waking up startled, panicking, but no one knew how close they had come to the annihilation of the earth, nor did they know about the demise of young Phaethon. In time, they would be grateful for the miracle of his transition to a new source of life-giving water.

That is the trouble with immortality: it makes it easy for gods to thrive, judge, demand, entertain themselves, or punish, often unaware of the pain or blessing they brought to mortal households. Perhaps mortals who experienced the consequences were lucky to have a limited time on earth, bearing all the pain and joy life allotted them.

THIRTEEN

MOURNING PHAETHON

L ightning had struck, the earth shook, and thunder crashed three times just minutes before Iris, Hera's herald, appeared inside Helios's marble halls. She had traveled from Mount Olympus on a rainbow path to deliver the news to Clymene, crossing smoky skies during the lingering twilight hours. Hera's handmaiden carried her rod, her hair and tunic covered with the boy's ash, and ignored the palace servants who ran to see what the commotion was. She rushed to Clymene's bedroom.

Iris resented having to be the bearer of sad news, but it was her lot to serve Hera and follow her instructions. It was the boy's youth and Zeus's rushed intervention that weighed on her this time. She had said as much to Hera, who agreed when they were alone. Rushing along the long hallways, she floated up the grand staircase, glowering at the waking household. Some servants were still rubbing their eyes, awakened by Zeus's and Iris's commotion. But no one knew yet about Phaethon's fate and the gravity of the news she was about to deliver. Entering the bedroom, she watched a startled Clymene leap out of bed and wrap herself in a white sheet.

She waited for the drowsy woman to wake up and recognize her presence. When Phaethon's mother focused her eyes on her, Iris saw the fright in the woman's eyes. The winged goddess bowed before delivering the chilling news simply and directly, just as Hera had instructed her.

"Dear Clymene, I am Iris, goddess of the rainbows, here to deliver Hera's message. Your precious son, the prince of the House of Helios, is no more! First in ash and then in thick liquid drops, Phaethon fell from Helios's chariot and is now quenching the thirst of our scorched earth. New rivers and rivulets are his tears." Iris's voice drifted off as Clymene froze, her expression turning wild.

"You cannot mean . . ." The terrified mother's voice was gripped with horror.

Iris set a hand softly against the woman's shaking body. "Lightning flashed three times and struck him," she explained, as carefully as she could. "It was from Zeus's hand, and Phaethon's death was instant. Hera sent me to tell you." She leaned closer and whispered, "The mother of all is so sorry. She shares in your sorrow, knows your pain. My heart goes out to you. My mistress may visit you soon."

"But why?" Clymene gasped. "Why?" she shrieked.

Iris took a step back. "The twilight was fading when Phaethon rode his father's chariot and lost control. Your boy was about to destroy the earth, setting fires." She gestured sadly, pointing out the windows lit by nearby simmering fires, and her voice softened. "Zeus had no choice." The messenger knew she had to fashion her words to show respect for the actions of the father of all.

She heard a sob escape Clymene's chest. Having accomplished her errand, the messenger fluttered her wings and vanished as quickly as a fading rainbow. Iris was unwilling to witness what was to come. Departing in the gloom, she supposed that all the women of the sun-god's palace and even people in nearby homes heard Clymene's piercing cries, howling her grief. Outside, there was silence, no chirping birds or crickets, as nature made room for her cries.

When Perse rose that morning, startled by the lightning and thunder, she lingered in her rooms before realizing what palace maids whispered excitedly, "Phaethon is dead. Zeus killed him."

"Hush! How do you dare start such rumors?" she demanded.

"He stole Helios's chariot."

"Hera's messenger came to tell Clymene."

"Yes, it was Iris."

"It's true. He is gone."

The queen tore through the palace, questioning everyone in her way, increasingly outraged. She pushed aside those who had poured into her sister's rooms.

"Clymene!" she cried, finding her sister curled up into a tiny pulp between sobs and shrieks, her body convulsing, exhausted. "Is it true? Iris has come . . . Phaethon?" She saw that Clymene's eyes were wild with pain; she needed no other confirmation and tried to soothe her, embrace her, cuddle her, but her sister jerked away. Phaethon's mother had been pulling out tufts of her graying hair.

Pushing Perse away, she shouted, "What is my life worth without my son? Let me die! Let me burn in a pyre to liberate my soul."

Perse shushed her, took out her handkerchief to wipe her sister's forehead and eyes, and saw Clymene was trying to scratch her cheeks, digging in with her nails. The queen reached out, embraced her again, and called out to her servant, "Melpomene, bring me warm water and more handkerchiefs. And inform Helios." Turning to the intruders and the curious, she ordered sharply, "Out. Leave us alone at once! Only Melpomene can be here."

When the evening fell over her rooms, Clymene, who by then was tearing her clothes and covering her hair in ashes, started howling again. Around her quarters hovered the air of despair and doom. The palace and village women had been gathering at the entrance of the palace. They had heard the news and had come to sing dirges demanding the world to stay still, calling out the boy's name. They sang:

> *Phaethon is gone! Young Phaethon!*
> *Our days are dark and stilled is the moon.*
> *His mother's heart is broken.*
> *His father's light is dim.*
> *Gone is the life of the palace.*

One servant in Clymene's room shouted angrily about the son's betrayal of his mother, about how he ignored her advice, his father's trust, his teacher's warnings. Outraged, Phaethon's mother lunged to tear her eyes out. It was Perse who kept them apart, sending the woman away. It was too soon for Clymene to see the truth in that.

She had to mourn the only way she knew how: all alone, hiding from the world, behind a veil of grief and anger, sinking into despair. Her sister stood by her for long hours, but finally, that evening, she went to find Helios and sent him to Clymene.

The day had been dark, leaving mortals and gods alike unsettled, cold, and shivering. The all-seeing Helios was brooding, pacing at the stables, thinking about fate. He visualized the Moirai in their hovel, sitting around a fire, contemplating every newborn's lifeline and future. They were to blame for what they granted his son! It was their fault.

They had promised the boy so much but had delivered Phaethon's premature demise and a lifetime of pain to his mother—and all because the Moirai had endowed him with ambition and an obsession with horses. Helios was mourning his son and his beloved team of horses. Clotho had certainly spun Phaethon a short life. The sun-god imagined her thin, long fingertips spinning into fibers, making threads, pulling on them to make them longer—but fragile, thin. It was her sister, heartless Lachesis, who had seized his life, measured its length, and pointed out where to cut it short.

The sun-god begrudgingly started on his daily trek late, relieving his waiting sister Eos from a lengthy shift. From his post, on a solitary horse, he rode between walks and trots, forgetting to wear his headdress. Approaching Mount Olympus, Helios heard Zeus tell his companions, "I don't blame the father. He tried to dissuade his son from riding his horses prematurely. He wanted to avoid an accident. But I had to stop the boy. I had to save the earth!"

Helios saw Apollo resting, sipping ambrosia from a golden cup, and heard him agree with Zeus. "Had he known what Phaethon planned, he would have intervened and prevented this tragedy. His disobedient son brought this onto himself."

Churning, anguished, the sun-god avoided greeting them. *There were a million ways Zeus could have responded: freeze him and the horses to give me time to intervene, force a landing, order him to return home . . .* Holding his tongue, he kicked his horse to canter on, wishing the day to be over. He knew it would be pointless to argue with the mighty Zeus, but he could not help feeling resentment. Grateful to Hera for giving some meaning to his son's life, he promised himself to offer a sacrifice after the funeral rites.

In the evening, upon Perse's urging, he came to Clymene's rooms, sending Melpomene away to have some private time with the mother of his son. Seeing him, Clymene ran to lean on his chest, seeking comfort, breaking out in a new deluge of tears.

"I can see his soft baby face. I feel him in my arms," she sobbed, sounding exhausted. "He will never fade; all the years I rocked him to sleep, petted his rosy cheeks, full of health, and saw in his eyes his dreams and acts of heroism—all burned in flames by Zeus's hand. How can anyone worship gods like ours?" she cried.

"He was our sweet son," was at first all the sun-god would say. The wrath of Zeus was well-known, so Helios kept his anger concealed, for he knew Zeus's power and decisiveness. Finally he added, "The father of all does not blame us."

He held Clymene tightly, feeling her sobs still racking her body, and then he let his tears trickle down as he rocked her gently.

Hour after hour and for the next few days, a crowd stood by, paying homage as the household dirges went on, lamenting the boy's demise. Several women had formed a daily circle around Clymene, keeping a constant vigil. Mostly they remained silent, because they understood that for Phaethon's mother the worst was that there was no body to prepare for the funeral. How was she to believe what had happened? It was too early to find solace in Hera's last-minute intervention.

At the temple, preparations were feverish for the boy's funeral rites and the final procession.

When at last all was ready, Helios led the crowd, on foot, proud, silent, wrapped in a purple chiton, wearing his crown, and holding a whip. Clymene, Perse, and other minor celestials, among them Selene and Eos, accompanied him a step behind. Clymene contained her grief, walking bent over on the path of the procession to witness last rites in absentia of her son's body. Stooped, dressed in black, wearing a heavy mourning veil over her face, she leaned on Perse's arm, the two moving in lockstep behind Helios toward the temple. Her love and grief for Phaethon were spilling out in silent tears.

The curious crowd noticed the queen wore no veil. Wrapped in a simple black tunic, she held her head high, her long hair in a roll with a barrette. Some whispered what they had heard from Leonora, who helped dress her before the procession. It was a queen's way of protesting the cruel act of Zeus.

Young boys, led by Phaethon's friend Orion and a dozen palace guards, scattered purple flowers and petals. Burning incense, the priest and temple servants lined up behind the royals and the boys; then came people from surrounding villages, drifting along. Leading the temple people, the head priest carried two golden cups. One contained a few of Phaethon's ashes meticulously gathered by the temple servants. The second cup contained water collected from a young river, thanks to Hera's intervention, the meager remains of a young, proud boy who did not reach his prime.

Following Helios's instructions, they stopped before the temple steps where the high priest poured libations to Zeus. Silence fell over the crowd when the priest chanted a brief public prayer on behalf of the palace:

> Praises be to Zeus, protector of the earth, master of
>   the starry heaven.
> Keep us safe from winds and thunderstorms and grant us
>   solace.
> Release Phaethon's spirit to the earth, grant him rest.

Turning toward the altar, he raised and carefully rested both cups on the marble and continued, offering praises to Charon.

He prayed that Charon would carry Phaethon over calm waters and, once they had peacefully crossed over the River Styx, deliver him to rest in the Elysian Fields.

There were more praises for the steady ferryman of souls, extolling his gentle ways, reminding him that Phaethon was the beloved prince of Helios's palace, that his people and family mourned the loss. The priest begged Charon to remain gentle, to be the steady guide of Phaethon's shadow as the boy entered the underworld:

> *Fates doomed him to an early death.*
> *We mourn with Clymene and our beloved master.*
> *Even gone from this world, he leaves behind gifts*
> *Of rivers and brooks sustaining life.*
> *We praise and will remember him forever.*

Slowly, the crowd gathered around a pyre assembled close to the temple. Approaching it, another priest carried a torch from inside the temple and lit it up. As the flames built up, dancing high, a chorus of women and temple servants cried out their mournful funerary hymns, calling out the boy's name: "Phaethon! Dear Phaethon, Young Phaethon, Doomed Phaethon!"

More chants praised Helios. Others begged for courage for Phaethon's mother and her bleeding heart. At Perse's request, they finished with praises to Hera for intervening. Phaethon's liquid grave would feed the earth, and his demise would not be for naught.

The crowd waited until the fire died down. Curious eyes kept on Clymene, who remained regal; she moved to lean on Helios's arm, and when the last hymn faded, the couple retreated to the palace, and the crowd dispersed for another cloudy day of mourning.

The evening after the funeral services, Helios sought solitude in his quarters. He had resumed his daily trek, delivering another short, overcast day. The world was gloomy and worried about the unseasonal darkness, disturbed by the dim light and cool temperatures. Some mortals had even come to temples and offered libations to Helios.

The sun-god was lying in his bed, staring at the ceiling, when Perse finally found him. He felt haggard. "It's you!" he said in a colorless voice.

He watched the queen's eyes spark even before she spoke and worried: *This is not simply grief.* He returned her gaze queryingly, sensing her anger about the cruelty of Zeus's last-minute panic intervention that led to Phaethon's death.

"Zeus stole our Phaethon!" she shouted. "You well know he did not have to become a destroyer!"

Perse was a troublemaker; she had no fear, no mercy, and no consideration for the consequences of her blasphemy to his household. He sat up, looking directly at her, and said, "Careful, wife. Remember, Hera saw to it that my boy has left his mark. People will love him for it." He turned his back to her but did not invite her to stay.

"I am not leaving until I hear how you will reclaim your place in the world," she said, moving to the window. "You are Helios Hyperion. I watched you staring at the running brooks and the glimmering new rivers. Your son is gone, but you are still the master of the skies. Claim your place with the Olympians! Make this house proud. Where is your courage?"

He sighed. "You have a lot more pluck, Perse, but I am exhausted. I need to rest."

When he turned in her direction again, she was quietly sitting by the window. She seemed thoughtful, but he worried she was pondering irreverent, perhaps even defiant, ideas. Deep down, he shared her anger but did not want to express it aloud. His wife was a strong woman. She had a temper; she inspired in him feelings of fright and admiration.

When she finally spoke, she sounded calm and settled. "You need to shine bright, claim your place," she demanded, "and so do we, your women. You are not alone, husband."

What he wished for was that she would temper her anger and accept divine guidance that would open a channel in her mind, a road to help Clymene heal and to find a lasting solution to Selene's troubles.

FOURTEEN

OLIVE HARVEST

*E*ach year, Perse relished the summer months, overseeing the gathering of olives, grapes, and luscious fruit that awaited the harvest. In the past it had been easy to forget her worries during the busy season, but this year Phaethon's loss and the price it took on Clymene distressed her. She had watched her sister leave the palace, taking frequent strolls alone by the olive orchard. She had heard her expressing her sorrow when she listened to trickling brooks or lingered by the young river that ran through the old grove. One day Clymene told Perse that she noticed the olives were about ready to pick.

The next day, at high noon, the queen found her sister at the olive grove still wearing a black veil tightly covering her head. She followed her to the rushing currents of a young river that was watering the thirsty grove. "It's my son's footprint, all he has left me. I love the sound of rushing water," said Clymene, settling next to the riverbank.

Perse, who loved the resonance of lapping water whenever she walked by riverbanks, knew it was the soothing sound that calmed and fed her sister's spirit and inspired her poetry. Her tone was soft when she continued, "We are water nymphs after all, dear Clymene. Bless Hera, who intervened, turning

Phaethon's death into a gift for you, his mother, and for Mother Earth and the living."

She watched Clymene bring out her handkerchief to dry a tear and listened to her speak. "I think of him each time servants light the palace torches with olive oil from our grove and when I dip my bread in food. This will be an ample harvest for many crops. Mortals should thank and recognize him."

Perse nodded, sat next to her sister, and shifted their conversation to shared memories of past harvests. "When my children, Circe and Aeetes, were a few years old, their father sometimes took them for rides on his chariot. He drove it proudly, making room for his tiny passengers, who held on to the carriage, barely tall enough to view the vista below." Perse imagined the chariot weaving over and under clouds and young Circe marveling at viewing patches of green, brown, and blue, and people with hats and headscarves bent over, working the fields and orchards, gathering crops.

"Circe told me how much she loved riding with her father; it was a thrill for her. My Phaethon did not enjoy such rides," Clymene said, tearing up again, "but you are right. Watering fields and valleys, he gifts the living richer crops."

Interrupting her, Perse rushed in with excitement in her voice, "Did you ever hear about Circe's reaction when her father rode over olive groves—when she witnessed mortals holding switches in their hands, people beating olive trees? Upset that the gnarled and twisted trunks and leafy branches were receiving such harsh punishment, she asked her father, 'What have the trees done to these mortals to get this treatment?'" Perse watched a smile rising on Clymene's lips and broke out in laughter. "Her father explained to her," the queen continued, "'They are gathering liquid gold, little one. It's worth the toil.'"

"Why don't you invite my favorite niece to join us here for

this olive harvest?" Clymene suggested. "I well remember her and miss her."

It was a relief for Perse to see her sister's eyes brighten, leaving gloomy thoughts behind, even momentarily, showing some spark and interest. "I shall," she promised. "During harvest, the three of us can join and pay tribute to Demeter, the goddess of fertile earth, and recognize Phaethon's gift to the earth, to mortals."

As soon as they returned to the palace, Perse rushed to her quarters and sent a homing pigeon to Aeaea, Circe's island, to deliver an invitation to the harvest rites.

Later, she shifted into a long sky-blue peplos and asked Leonora to bring her a tiara and a necklace of lapis beads. Then Perse rejoined her sister in the Great Hall, entering with the usual fanfare. Worrisome news had been traveling among the courtiers about a new battle that was breaking out in Athens. Minos, the king of Crete, had put a call forward to form an army to fight against the Athenians. It would travel to the continent to invade and conquer new lands.

"What is that all about? It is often humans encouraged by gods," Perse declared, her hands folding again into fists, "that instigate new wars."

Helios did not disagree. "Ares, the god of war, had urged the king's advisers to encourage him with flattery and ambition to seek more wealth and power."

At the thought of the slaughter of battles and the flames of war, the queen protested, "No matter the cause, it's a horrendous, pointless loss of life. There *has* to be another way."

Clymene said, "More mothers will grieve."

Yet a few of Helios's guards were agitating; some courtiers whose heritage was from those parts were even talking about joining the faraway army for glory and loot.

"I would rather celebrate life"—Perse glared at the palace

guards—"enjoy the harvest and join my sister and niece observing the rites of living earth and creation." Turning to Clymene, she added, "I already sent a message for Circe to join us, sister."

The queen looked away and scratched her temple thoughtfully. Problems and possible answers were swirling in her mind, but primary was resolving Selene's entanglements and soothing Zeus's anger for her sister-in-law's transgressions.

Hyperion Helios, all knowing as he was, shared with his wife and Clymene, "Zeus is grateful to Hera for intervening and redirecting him to turn Phaethon into a life-giving source of rivers and brooks."

Perse had recognized that, deep down, her husband was relieved that the father of all had not rebuked him for his son's behavior. Was he feeling guilty for paying minimal attention to his boy? No matter, Zeus had even encouraged them to assure that mortals recognized and paid tribute to Phaethon for the blessings of water.

Circe, the enchanted daughter of Helios and Perse, had not seen her aunt since Clymene had hosted them—herself, her mother, and her brother Aeetes—long ago in Ethiopia when Phaethon was still a toddler. She had learned the news of her cousin's demise from Hecate.

When the homing pigeon delivered her mother's invitation, Circe, who had been sore at Perse, attempted to ignore it. She considered her mother puzzling. In the recent past, Perse had promised her daughter to return to Circe's island and join in the special annual festivities honoring the arts and local talent. She had never turned up. Now her mother's message read: *Come to Helios's palace. My sister Clymene is mourning Phaethon's loss and needs our help. We can engage her in the olive harvest rites. She would welcome your presence, dear daughter.*

Circe blinked and felt her old resentments rise up. Growing

up, the enchantress resented her mother's constant need to show off and felt that she had never gained her approval. Why should she even respond? Nervously, she crumpled the message between her fingers, finally running her palm over it, flattening and rereading it. She would not have made the effort for her mother, who had been critical of her in the past, but she had fond memories of her aunt. The enchantress considered the invitation overnight, and out of a sense of compassion for her mourning aunt she scribed her acceptance in the morning and sent it back with the pigeon. Her inquisitive nature propelled her to overcome her hesitation. Her mother might have changed with age. She knew *she* had. And her aunt needed her.

The sorceress had taken to shape-shifting for travel. A week later, a majestic raptor landed in Perse's garden, her mighty talons wrapped around the branches of an oak tree. Peering inside the queen's quarters, Circe's eagle eyes focused on the unsuspecting Perse, who was working at her perfume table. Noisily, she skipped to the ground, bathed, and drank water from the fountain. Then she shifted back to her youthful form, shaking off her feathers. The yard filled with white, dark gray, and mottled plumage, and a startled Perse abandoned her perfumes and ran out to the garden to see what it was. Once Circe had shed all her feathers, she draped around her body a plain white peplos and a pearl necklace. Inside the satchel she carried gifts of lekythoi, decorated with images of bathing women, one for Clymene and another for her mother. She had filled them with bathing oils scented with juniper.

Recognizing her mother running down the stairs, Circe paused as the woman drew her in for an embrace. "Dear Circe, so glad you came! So elegant!" A couple of servants ran to collect the scattered feathers, and Leonora waited for orders.

Circe followed her mother to the fragrant part of the garden, and they sat under the jasmine tree. She felt Perse's eyes checking her head to toe, her eyes bright with glee. "So glad you are here!" she added. "Your father and aunt will be happy to see you. What would you like for Leonora to bring you?"

"More water, Mother. I am thirsty from the trip." Then she reached into her satchel and smiled. "Here, I brought you a small gift," she said, setting the lekythos on the table. It was an artfully crafted ceramic container and a guest offering, one Circe knew her mother would appreciate. "I have one for you and another for my aunt. I hope you like it."

Perse took it, uncorked it, sniffed, and smiled. "You remembered that juniper is one of my favorite fragrances! I love it!"

Circe downed a full cup of water, refilling it from the pitcher Leonora had brought, while Perse ordered her servant to prepare the bath and invite Clymene to join them. Then she shared with Circe, "Helios is preoccupied. He has been working long hours with Asim, the stable master, to train new teams of horses, hitching them to a brand-new chariot. "You will not see much of him," she warned. Finally, Perse spoke about Clymene. "Your aunt is having a hard time since her son's demise, dear Circe. I hope she will join us for the olive harvest rites. I hope she takes part. Do encourage her when you see her."

Later that day, Circe roamed on the first and second floors of the palace. Some spaces were the same, and others had changed. Lush gardens and new mosaics with more symbols of Helios on the floors, walls, and ceilings had been added. She admired new frescoes and mosaics of radiant eyes, bursts of rays, and scenes set during sunrise and sunset, but most hallways and rooms were familiar. She started for her childhood quarters, where she and her brother had been raised, and found the old frescoes depicting Oceanid nereids dancing, swimming, and playing with her brother and her young self. That space was now used by Clymene.

When she entered Clymene's bedroom, she found her aunt

still in bed, with her servant begging her to have some food. Clymene had refused to join the queen and her niece in taking a bath. Seeing Circe in her room, she raised herself on her elbows and stepped out of bed, embracing her and tearing up.

"My dear aunt," said Circe, hugging her back tightly and kissing her on both cheeks, "I have come to be with you." She lovingly straightened her aunt's graying, tangled hair and continued, "Mother has invited us to her baths any time you want to join us. Look what I brought you!" Then she reached into her satchel and handed her the lekythos.

Clymene dismissed the gift, and Circe set the lekythos on a nearby table. When her aunt returned to her bed, Circe frowned, startled by the deep dark circles around her aunt's eyes. Clymene clasped her breast. "Last night, as I was drifting to sleep, Phaethon's face slipped in." A deep sob rattled her chest, and Circe saw her eyes tear up again. "He lives in my heart, my dear. I die each night," she said, wiping her eyes with the back of her hand.

Although Hypnos had been sitting heavily on her eyelids, Phaethon's mother admitted to being tortured with frequent nightmares. She told her niece she would wake up startled and get up filled with dread, unable to sleep the rest of the night.

Circe saw the wisdom in her mother's plan to engage Clymene in the harvest rituals. She hoped her aunt would be willing to join. Following her mother's advice, she asked Clymene to take a walk with her to the olive grove. To that, Clymene agreed readily.

In the distant past, Perse had watched mortals gather for harvests and had led several field rituals to honor Demeter and Persephone, goddesses of agriculture. She respected the female Olympians, observed traditions, and frequently carried out tributes to them, always looking to develop alliances. Helios was too busy to join her in the local fields and orchards, for his mission was to bring daylight around the globe.

After Circe's arrival, the queen looked for Leonora in the kitchen. It was unusual for her to appear in that busy space. All the women's eyes followed her to the long table, where her faithful servant was leaning over a dish of lentils. Perse tapped her on her shoulder. "It's time to gather the olives, Leonora. We will start in a week, now that Circe is here. Tell Melpomene to encourage her mistress to join us."

Seeing her servant's raised eyebrows, Perse blinked, hesitated for a minute, and in a conciliatory tone added, "I should have spoken to you earlier, but it will be the usual ritual. We pay tribute to Demeter and Persephone, but most of all, I want to celebrate this occasion with my sister, my daughter, and our people. This year, during the days of harvest, we should remember and honor Phaethon for his life-giving gift of water. Once they know it comes from him, our people will appreciate and honor him."

Overhearing, some of the kitchen help groaned for the long nights of preparation, while others smiled, hoping they would get chosen to lend a hand to the harvest and leave the kitchen. Leonora said, "I was expecting the news." She looked around the room and shouted, "Let's get to work, girls! There is a lot to do." She was ready to hand out their assignments.

The next morning, Circe found Clymene walking on uneven ground following the lineup of trees to the large olive grove. The silver leaves were shimmering in the morning breeze. The two women synchronized their steps down the gentle hillside. Dressed informally in short tunics and sandals, they tiptoed toward the new river, away from the formalities of the Great Hall.

Green olives dotted the leafy branches of the trees. Once they reached the river, Clymene knelt, scooped some water into her palm, and drank a sip. "I do this every time," she confessed, and applied the rest of the water to her face. "Refreshing! Try it," she urged her niece.

Circe copied her aunt and remained kneeling. "A blessing for men and gods! The thirst-quenching Phaethon remains eternal and will stay with us as long as there is life. We bless the water and are blessed by his presence, my dear aunt. You must be so proud of him!"

"Look at how plump the olives are, ready for picking," said Clymene.

Circe stretched on her tiptoes, reaching to pick a few. "This year, I will join you in the harvest rites," she said, and offered one to Clymene.

Her aunt accepted the olive, smiled, and said, "That is good!"

FIFTEEN

HARVEST RITES

The opening celebrations always started early in the morning, with the crew assembling to enjoy a hearty first meal together. At the expanse next to one side of the palace, known as "Palm Grove," servants had covered the ground with blankets and trays heaped up with hearty foods. People from surrounding communities who were loyal to Helios and who would be in the work crews swarmed in to find an abundance of fruit, cheese, bread, honey, oats, and milk laid out for them.

Helios's three women agreed to join the crew at the end of the meal and mingle, meeting and greeting some of them. Perse had given her daughter and sister each a special set of hand-tooled leather sandals, head coverings (a black one for Clymene), and simple cotton tunics to keep them cool.

The queen was the first to arrive and made the rounds, chatting with people she recognized. Most of the crew had not heard that the enchantress, who arrived with Clymene, would be there. "We welcome divine Circe," they said.

Clymene received the warmest reception as some, aware of her son's newfound legacy, bowed, curtsied, and called out, "Hail, sweet mother of nourishing Phaethon."

When the crew finished their meal, they collected their

wares and followed the three royals down the dusty path to the orchard, carrying baskets, nets, switches, ladders, big jars, and small tools. The crew moved in clusters of two and three, keeping a pace.

Busy Leonora, Perse's chambermaid, was among the last to join, riding on a donkey loaded up with baskets and jars.

"How is your bottom doing, Leonora?" the handler asked her, chuckling.

"It's a long way to the orchard. Where would you rather be? On the road or on the donkey?" She laughed and winked. The kitchen maids nearby chuckled.

Leonora's relaxed mood led to more questions. "Were you ever married, Leonora?"

"If you find a man, you are happy. If you don't, you turn into a philosopher, like me," she said, smiling. It was a jolly crowd that continued to banter, tittering with conversations about life in Helios's country.

When they reached the olive grove, the crew laid the equipment in a pile at the edge of the orchard and cut olive branches from the trees, lining up in a procession to honor Demeter, the goddess of agriculture. Two by two, they walked to the middle of the field, forming a wide circle around their three leading goddesses.

In a booming voice, Perse offered thanks to Demeter for the crop they were about to gather, and the crowd responded to her words, repeating her praises in unison:

We are grateful to the ancient earth that gives us
*   sustenance.*
Nature's wonders are plentiful. Her gifts to us are rich.
Praises be to gracious Demeter who has blessed this harvest,
To Phaethon for nourishing the trees
Granting us another year of prosperity and peace.

The ceremony ended with Clymene pouring libations on the roots of the oldest olive tree and Circe tying colorful ribbons of gratitude on its lower branches, which signaled the beginning of the harvest. From there, the crew moved into the olive grove, spread their nets underneath the trees, and rested the ladders against the tree trunks. In the afternoon, when the setup was finished, Helios's women took switches and waited for everyone to hold theirs in their hands. Then Perse led them with a song that had a distinct downbeat. Following the rhythm, they began beating the olive branches. Their words urged the trees to release their fruit gently to the ground. They sang the refrain three times:

Olive groves in Demeter's glory
Blessed be our harvest story.
Green, brown, black, and honey gold.
Pray that it be ninefold.

Hera's encouragement, the physicality of the activity, and the group synergy under blue skies and sunny days lifted Clymene's spirits. She joined, humming along.

As she finished uttering the last word, Clymene rested her eyes on a newfound spring that had been quenching the workers' thirst all morning. She wiped a tear that escaped down her cheek as her chest swelled with a bundle of pain. Her son's demise was an aching loss, although in other eyes, he had joined Mother Earth to feed life.

She had done all she could, raising a troublesome son, and she missed him, but there was more to consider. *It is always women who bear the brunt of keeping things on an even keel*, she thought. *I have gone along with all the Fates have handed me, but there is no room left to spare.* After all, she needed to take care of herself and attend to her own soul. For today, it was time to return to the palace and rest.

The olive harvest kept Helios's royal women busy from September through November. They walked around the grove off and on, content with progress. Toiling alongside the crews of mortals, they gathered olives from the nets set on the ground and complained about the hot September days. They would stop to rest in the shade to have a drink of water and thank the people for their hard work.

Clymene's mood lightened, thanks to the chatter of workers, the activity, and Circe's companionship. On days when she stayed in the palace, she sometimes watched the girls in the kitchen prepare jars for the cellar. She would interrupt them with questions about how much oil they produced and how they refined it for cooking. On most days, though, the kitchen help answered her while washing and scoring each olive with a sharp knife and then curing the olives in brine and vinegar, adding spices to make special, delectable treats just as Helios liked them. Tangy and a little bitter, the olives were served year-round on a platter for evening meals, next to slices of cheese drizzled with olive oil.

As for Perse, satisfied that all was moving along smoothly at the olive grove, she turned her attention to palace affairs and Selene's heartaches and kept cajoling reluctant Helios to deliver Hera's demands to Selene. The moon goddess's decision was overdue and necessary. At the Great Hall, in his chamber, at the stables, and whenever she met him, she would press him with, "Have you an answer from your sister, my husband? She cannot delay any longer."

One day, Circe and Clymene accidentally found their way to a room that served as an oil press. Certainly no place for royal visitors, it was dark and noisy. When they heard grinding sounds and the braying of animals, they were intrigued and followed men carrying baskets of olives. In the center of the room, a huge round granite stone, resting in a bowl, was crushing green olives into pulp to make virgin oil. The stone rolled over the fruit that had been tossed in, powered by a harnessed donkey walking in circles around the granite bowl. Clymene tracked the pulp being channeled into a pit below, half filled with water, and rested her eyes on the golden liquid floating over the water. After a pause, turning to her niece, she spoke pensively, thrilled to witness the process. "My dear, in time pure oil separates and floats to the surface and the dregs fall to the bottom. It is not always easy to sort out what is important to hold on to in life." She had cried, dreamed, talked to family, written poems, and contemplated her loss and her own life; it had been a slow and painful process.

"I should be appreciative for life and health, and shoulder what hardships the Olympians hand me. My son's passing has been a stab in my heart. Yet I should be grateful for my family that has surrounded me patiently with love; thank you, my dear." Her eyes were shining. She reached out to Circe, and the women embraced.

Thrilled to hear her aunt make a breakthrough from the dark days of mourning, Circe knew she could leave Helios's palace after the final harvest rites, relieved her aunt was mending and willing to accept support. "Kin can be like the oil that fuels our torches at night, dear Clymene, that sheds light and gives another perspective. I am grateful for you and our family."

SIXTEEN

SELENE'S LAST HURDLES

*H*elios met his sister at that thin veil of time between sunset and darkness. He was riding an exact copy of his destroyed chariot with the new team of horses. He slowed them down and waited for Selene to appear. The sun-god noticed an umbra of a dark, starless night spreading behind her.

She slowed down to ask, "How is your family? You? How is Clymene?"

He leaned toward her chariot until their eyes met. "Clymene is having a hard time. Thank goodness Circe is here. It helps." He sensed she was studying him.

Selene said, "Zeus has been listening to the cruel Fates, handing off death sentences. We lost your son. A harsh ending. And then the slaughter of mortals. Minos is assembling an army that soon leaves for the Athenian battlefields, sailing north; he, too, will leave behind mothers moaning the slaughter of their sons and husbands."

He thought her eyes were sparking with anger. "Dear sister, you are aware that our family is not in Zeus's favor anymore after Phaethon's treacherous death. He will not give you more time.

Your lover's days will be over soon. You know there is nothing you can do unless Endymion accepts Eos's proposal. Has our sister spoken to you?" His younger team of horses was getting restless; he usually was a man of few words. Helios pulled the reins tight to keep the team steady and listened to her answers.

"I have spoken to him in passing. I must say, he still hopes to get his way, a full life and eternity." He could hear her swallowing hard.

"He cannot have that. You need a final decision, or he will regret hesitating. He is in peril." Though he did not like to, Helios forced himself to use words that dripped with danger to assure that his sister heard the alarm. Selene had to accept the fact that the gods were tired of waiting for her to end the affair, and he was not about to support her.

"I will soon," she promised. "I just need a day or two."

His sister had finally heard him! "A day or two then," he repeated, draping his tunic tighter to his body against a chill, and loosened the reins. He was on his way home.

The following night, she did not return to Mount Latmus. Selene arranged to meet Lampetia and Phaethusa on their island of Trinacia. Early that evening, she landed on the rocky west side of the island, on top of a striated cliff face that dropped into the sea. Her winged steeds found the flat landing where her nieces waited in front of a shallow cave with an arched opening.

Selene wore a dark blue peplos with a gold pendant that was Helios's present. She found Lampetia and Phaethusa watching her dismount. They greeted her with embraces, eager to show her the surprise they had arranged. They had commissioned a craftsman from Helios's palace who worked on this deserted corner of the island to emblaze Selene's favorite symbol over the cave's entrance. The goddess saw her own pale light reflecting the carved shape of a crescent moon, inlaid with citrine.

"It will be easier to find this spot," said her nieces with one voice.

She nodded, and a bitter smile formed on her face for an instant. "Thank you. A fitting mark for my lover's future mausoleum." An unexpected release of tension followed her sigh.

Phaethusa and Lampetia led the way inside. The ceiling was low, and a torch gently lit the space. A glass roof window opened the view to the sky and a slice of the Milky Way. Over the center of the cave rose a solid block of flat rock, smooth and wide enough to hold two bodies. Selene ran her hand across the top.

"We will need soft pillows and sheepskins to rest him on," said Selene. "I will bring some when I return." Overcome with emotion, she turned her back to her nieces, holding back tears. "The end of fine days, soon to turn into memories," she murmured.

Lampetia rushed next to her. "Shepherds come through here every morning and just before sunset, once they have settled Helios's herds. They will keep watch over him. And you can come whenever you want. No one will bother you when you visit, dear Selene."

"Love does not end. It turns into fond memories," Phaethusa added. "Zeus will defeat gods and mortals, but not our memories."

Selene drew a deep breath and smiled. It was reassuring to see there was a place for him and know her nieces had thought about his care. It seemed fitting that he would rest among shepherds. She could be an inconspicuous visitor during this transition. The moon goddess would soon be thrust into living between the *before* and the *after*. She was glimpsing another chapter of her journey, but she was not yet ready to start over and reinvent herself. For the moment, she could not fathom what it might look like.

What would Endymion choose? Would he agree to accept the gift of eternity, remaining frozen in a state of sleep? And what if he did not? He might see eternal sleep as punishment. If that was his reaction, she would have to live with guilt for his untimely near-death, knowing she had taken all his youthful days.

But then, what was this lightness she felt, this sense that old straps no longer bound her, that she could venture out and explore new corners of the sky, have fresh encounters with mortals and gods? Her brother was right to be after her this time. She called them and her winged steeds moved toward her. As she climbed into her chariot, an odd-sounding laugh slipped out of her lips. She rocked back and forth and called out, "Giddyap!"

Thereafter, the night was dark, the quarter moon hiding behind heavy clouds. On Mount Latmus Selene's lover was waiting outside the cave when her winged steeds landed. Endymion helped her dismount and settled the steeds.

"I missed you last night." He ran his eyes down her curvy body and then noticed the dark shadows around them. "I am sorry about the hard days of mourning Phaethon. How is your family?"

"My brother and Phaethon's mother are devastated. How could Zeus . . ." She did not finish. It was not wise to criticize the father of all again.

The shepherd held his arms out, reaching for her waist, but she ignored him and entered the cave, saying, "But we have troubles of our own. Zeus has been expecting your response. Have you thought about what fate you prefer? Few get to choose between death or life in eternal sleep."

He watched her settle on a low bench, then sat on the floor covered with sheepskins, his legs akimbo. "What a way to start our time together! You are funny!" He tossed his curls away from his eyes and forced a snicker. Endymion picked up a ceramic cylix, poured red wine from a goatskin askoi, and handed it to Selene. She took it, cut it with water, and held it.

Her voice sounded steely to his ears, her look direct. "We have run out of time, my dear. You must believe me. If you do not choose, you will wake up in Hades, a shadow of yourself, and lost to me forever."

He felt his breath stop short, coughed, and shuddered at the thought of the labor of death. The awful choice was obvious, but he was not ready to speak it. The weight of the decision drained his energy. He pressed her again, "You can ask him to grant me eternity, Selene, one more time. Zeus has favored you in the past, for you softened many nights, shedding pale rays for his romantic moments, helping him in his trysts and conquests."

She pointed toward Mount Olympus and said, "Zeus is giving you a choice. Take it, Endymion!"

The shepherd pressed his temples between his hands, feeling dizzy. Could he lose his mind? "You are killing me slowly, my love. How can you do that?" Fear overtook him, as he realized Olympian Zeus's patience must be exhausted. *What was the choice again? Death and Hades or immortality—but immortality in a lingering state of sleep?*

He had to concede that eternity in hibernation was his better option. Still, he moved behind her, reaching to embrace her, but felt her body stiffen. Tugging at her, he grasped her hands, then knelt and started kissing them.

Selene pushed him away, set her cylix on the floor, and started for her chariot. "After Phaethon's cruel demise, I am drained; there is no goodwill between Zeus and me. You need to give me your answer tomorrow."

Thunderclaps from an impending storm raging in the distance accompanied Selene's return the next night. She arrived wearing the same dark blue peplos and her brother's pendant, feeling the burden of an imminent ending and hoping to find Endymion's resignation to his fate. She longed for a quick resolution. She dismounted and realized he was standing outside, by the mouth of the cave, tall and unkempt, greeting her with, "My cruel love is back."

Flinching, she countered, "Eternal life and eternal sleep. That is what I hope you have chosen, my Endymion." Her voice softened. "I would rather you held on to life and eternity. Even an endless sleep is better than Hades."

She felt him staring for a long time before responding with a sigh. "Even asleep, I will know it when you come to me. My heart will beat faster. Perhaps I was arrogant to want an eternal life with you. I will wait for you to come at night. Will you come?"

She did not answer, could see his resignation and anguish, yet she felt relief that he had made his choice. Most of all, she wanted to ensure that he was in a safe place and left alone and unburdened. Would she ever be free of this time? But this was no time to expose her vulnerabilities.

He was blessed in a cruel way, spared the angst of old age, illness, and impending death. At least he would not be one of those needlessly killed by the victorious armies of battling Greeks. Some aspect of Endymion, not yet clear to either of them, would linger on.

"Where will I be?" He narrowed his eyes and grasped her hand, as a clap of lightning lit the sky.

"There is a quiet cave in Trinacia, an island where Helios's daughters mind his herds. It is a special place, under my protection, a place shepherds pass through each morning and afternoon. They will tend to you each day. It is a muted place, and I will visit you . . ."

Another thunderclap roared and then three strikes of lightning. Selene stopped. From Mount Olympus, the thundering voice of Zeus affirmed, "It will be so!" He had been listening in.

SEVENTEEN

THE END OF HARVEST

That night, the scrying mirror Perse kept by her bedside came to life. It was Hecate this time. Having witnessed Selene's visit to Trinacia and Zeus's consent, the sorceress hurried to relay the news to Helios's wife.

An ecstatic Perse rushed in then, interrupting her husband's sleep to share the excellent report her trusty ally had delivered. Lifting the tapestry between their rooms, she slipped into his bed and woke Helios up, despite his annoyance for her midnight raids. "What's wrong?" he asked, startled and groggy.

The queen honeyed her voice to soothe him. "The goddess of the moon listened to you, my husband. Well done! Your daughters and Selene will move Endymion to the mausoleum they prepared. Selene is safe from Zeus's wrath."

"How do you know?" He yawned, rubbed his eyes, and turned to look at her.

"Hecate messaged me. The plan worked! Hera has delivered another miracle!"

He smiled and pulled her toward his chest. "You are my miracle queen."

Perse felt his lips brush against her neck and ears. His arms felt strong, inviting, and she was ready to slip into his embrace.

She set aside what she had planned to pepper him with, about the growing wave of young men, Orion among them, who talked about joining Minos's army to fight in Athens. Shutting her eyes, she sighed and, hungry for a night of passion, climbed onto his chest.

The crews had been toiling for two months, and the last days of gathering olives were drawing near. Circe and Clymene had kept Perse updated about the harvest progress. Workers were accustomed to seeing the royals mingle and greet them in familiar ways. In turn, they offered courtesies: a seat in the shade, cold water from a nearby spring, curtsies, and smiles. In the late afternoons, the royals welcomed Leonora's and Melpomene's ministrations of aromatic baths and tasty meals, and rested from the toil of the day, catching up with court gossip.

Perse had asked Circe to keep track of time, using her wand to carve lines into a tall, flat rock that stood in the middle of the orchard. It was filling up with little room left near the top, a signal to all that they were nearing the end of harvest. The day Perse saw that Circe had carved the final line, she planned to deliver the last rites of worship for Demeter and called on Leonora to orchestrate "a boisterous community celebration for the crew with a hearty meal, song, and merrymaking."

The harvest had been rich; people were tired and grateful for the bounty. But there was unrest among some young men who wanted to leave Helios's service. They were agitating: "You do not need us past the end of the harvest." Perse was concerned, but she knew they wouldn't dare leave without Helios's consent.

It was the queen's duty to conduct the final harvest rites. On the designated day, wearing for the last time her well-worn, tattered summer sandals, frayed by the rocky paths and daily labor, Perse took the long, dusty path to the olive grove. She was joined by Clymene and Circe. The people greeted them as they passed by, and the royals responded with praises:

"Grateful for your toil . . . Tonight we celebrate . . . Thanks be to Demeter, her daughter, and Phaethon . . ."

Once at the grove, Perse spent the morning examining the fruit collected in their baskets, applauding their hard work. At noon, she declared the harvest over. The queen, her sister, and her daughter invited the workers to gather around, and then, raising her arms to the sky, she called out:

Blessed be Demeter and Phaethon
For a plentiful year of harvest.
Green, brown, black, and honey gold.
Praises be, it was ninefold!

Hearing the call, the harvesters followed the three royals, who had gathered by the oldest olive tree ready to lead with the familiar paean to Demeter, one they sang every year. They crowded around the tree, forming a circle, their voices blending in harmony, and they repeated each line:

Hail, Demeter, mother of all, gentle goddess,
Hear our thankful prayer, lady of fruits and grains,
of rich soil and harvest rains.
Thank you for another plentiful harvest,
And the blessings you bring!
You who banish growth each winter,
And stir the land each spring.

Then Perse raised her voice again, offering a new praise as the crew repeated spontaneously, stealing looks at Clymene, who was staring at the sky.

Hail, Phaethon, for nourishing the earth,
With flowing rivers, ponds, and brooks,
Quenching the land's thirst
And gifting us fertile harvests and plump fruits.

As the crew repeated the words, Perse's gaze turned toward Clymene. She saw tears well up in her sister's eyes. They embraced for a moment of shared sorrow and remembrance. Then Clymene covered her face with the black headscarf and silently took the path toward the palace.

Workers gathered their wares and scattered. Some were humming along tunes in anticipation of the evening celebration and others were busily checking the orchard, making sure they had picked up all the tools before starting for their homes.

In the evening, the crew trickled into the grove by the new river that stretched near the palace, spread out blankets, and settled down to wait for the plentiful food the cooks were about to bring out. Laughter and chatter filled the air as the aroma from the palace kitchens wafted in the air. It was a warm November evening, and palms surrounded the crew, heavy with honey-blonde dates, ready to be picked.

When Perse and Clymene withdrew to rest, Helios joined the gathering, mingling among the crew with Circe. People were in a merry mood, and their master was feeling generous. He asked those close by what they wanted for their reward.

"I want a day off to swim and rest," said the youngest, the most daring.

Another pair whispered to each other first, and then the oldest said shyly, "We each want a new tunic for festivals and days of celebration, dear master. Please, let us choose the cloth."

A sturdy young man with an athletic build asked, "Permission to leave the palace and join an army in Athens, my glorious master."

It was a moment of celebration and the sun-god, with no hesitation, promised to fulfill all their wishes. He raised his cylix, toasting, "To Zeus, Demeter, and Phaethon! I am thankful for the toil of all crews that sustain the world. And to my son for a very rich harvest." The whole gathering raised their cylices and sipped their wine.

As he did every year, he asked those who harmonized with the aulos to sing popular, sweet, and bawdy tunes about summer harvests and watched people take part as the spirit moved them. Some formed a circle and danced to rhythmic songs, twirling, clapping, and weaving among the diners.

Helios was not much for dancing tonight, so he returned to his rooms and lay on his bed to release the tension weighing down his limbs. Shutting his eyes, he tuned into his contemplative mind, emptying the chatter and quieting his thoughts. He found himself in a dreamy state, one filled with images. Notions of birth and death, the distillation of loss seized him. He had seen thousands of beginnings and as many endings on his daily route. Although immortal, he carried the weight of every day, the grief of loss and memories. Sometimes he found harbor in restful nights, but this was not one of them. His dreams returned to Phaethon and his fiery end.

Soon he would be up to begin his daily trek. The busy harvest season was over; the earth had delivered abundant crops and hope for a quiet and peaceful fall. People were turning a new leaf, bringing out heavier clothes, lighting the hearths to warm their homes, and gearing up for the snowy days of winter.

PART II

Let the bard sing what he has a mind to; bards do not make the ills they sing of; it is Jove [Zeus], not they, who makes them, and who sends weal or woe upon mankind according to his own good pleasure. This fellow means no harm by singing the ill-fated return of the Danaans, for people always applaud the latest songs most warmly. Make up your mind to it and bear it; Ulysses [Odysseus] is not the only man who never came back from Troy, but many another went down as well as he.

—Homer, *The Odyssey*,
Book 1.398–416 (trans. Samuel Butler)

EIGHTEEN

DEPARTURES

The days were getting shorter, rains filled brooks and rivers, trees shed their leaves, and winds whistled through the air. Circe, mistress of Aeaea, declared her intention to defy gravity once more and fly over the Aegean on mighty eagle wings to return home.

During her stay, she had developed a tender bond with her aunt Clymene and gained a deep respect for her mother's diligent caretaking efforts. She had witnessed Perse's purposeful efforts to reach out to Pacifae, her sister in distant Crete, to ensure she had been satisfied with the work of famed architect Daedalus. Most importantly, she had discovered she shared her mother's convictions against the war. They both saw it as an affliction they wished to defy and end, a stance her father was still ambivalent about. Perhaps a sisterhood of goddesses could resist the horrors of battlefields.

On her final night, Circe entered her mother's quarters to find Perse sitting by the dim light of oil lamps at her desk, clutching a small pouch. The queen welcomed her with open arms, drawing her close.

"My dear daughter, having you here has been a blessing, and it's hard to bid you farewell!" She handed Circe the pouch.

"It is only fitting that I pass on to you a cherished keepsake I received from your grandmother Tethys when you were born."

Circe, surprised by this gift, extracted a small object out of the pouch. The delicate amulet dangled from a golden chain. Moving closer to the torchlight at the other end of the room, the enchantress examined a beautifully crafted golden pendant. "It's exquisite and perfectly formed. Mother, is it a mandrake?"

"Indeed, it is the blossom of a mandrake plant. I adore its delicate ovate leaves and how the artist arranged them in a rosette, and of course you recognize it. You cultivate it in your herb garden. I sometimes use it in my perfumes for its multifaceted properties." Both women knew that different parts of the plant could be poisonous, provide pain relief, act as a narcotic or hallucinogenic, and even lead to madness.

Circe held the small object with reverence and kissed it. "Unknowingly, I have honored the knowledge and power of my ancestors. Thank you, Mother, for passing on to me this family heirloom from my grandmother! She, too, understood the potency and power of herbs. I will treasure it." Placing the pendant around her neck, she felt a warm ripple run through her body as it touched her breast. "I feel her blessing!" she affirmed.

"You are my extraordinary daughter," Perse replied, motioning for her to return and sit beside her once more.

It had been a fulfilling visit. Circe had witnessed her mother's unwavering determination and her sense of destiny as she tackled obstacles and sought alliances with like-minded goddesses and her three thousand Oceanid sisters. The enchantress now realized that this sisterhood could transform into a powerful network of support.

"Mother, have you talked with my father about Orion and the other young men? Will he permit them to go to war in Athens?"

"We are working to resolve it, my dear. Helios informs me he is in a difficult position. I plead with him and pray to Hecate, our dear goddess of light in darkness, to guide us toward an alternate path. But you know the Athenians murdered Androgeus, Minos's son, and the Cretan royals seek revenge."

"Why was he murdered?"

Perse recounted how Minos's son had triumphed in every contest of the Panathenaic Games hosted by Aegeus, the king of Athens. Instead of honoring him, jealous contestants had taken his life.

Circe felt her face twist in anguish, her hand rising to her heart in lightning anger. "Another young life lost! What is happening to our family?"

The queen sounded too reasonable. "I understand Minos and Pacifae's anger, their thirst for revenge. Yet we must dissuade them from another war. I am still working on it."

"There has to be another solution!" Circe exclaimed. "Soon, more lives will be lost, more bloodshed. More mothers will mourn their sons and husbands." In frustration, she sensed that if Orion and other young men were resolute to join Minos's army in Athens, Helios would not intervene.

"We are not the only ones who despise wars and all of the violent actions of Ares, the god of war," Perse said. "We need more than words to support peacemakers among us."

"Mother, I will gladly assist you to find new allies and create a circle of unity for peace. Your sisters and others will eagerly join. I know Clymene will be on board. We have to at least take a stance."

Perse reached out, gently tucking a stray curl behind Circe's ear, her eyes gleaming. "A Circle of Unity for Peace—this name has a beautiful ring to it. An excellent name for our network of goddesses! We will have our gatherings here once we have a proper space, my dear. Promise me you will come back!"

"Aeaea beckons me to make preparations for winter, but I will come back whenever you need me, Mother," Circe vowed.

On the morning of her departure, Helios waited for his daughter to shift shapes in her mother's garden and accompanied her, guiding his team of horses most of the way to Aeaea. The eagle with the piercing eyes and unwavering orientation thrived, traveling within the warm embrace of his protective rays. Circe returned to her island with a new sense of connection to her family.

Helios's royal house was also tracking the latest developments involving his sister. The family breathed a sigh of relief, watching Selene move Endymion to the care of shepherds on Lampetia and Phaethusa's island. On the appointed day, Zeus rendered Endymion immobilized and paralyzed. Hypnos, the gentle god of sleep, rested on his shoulder and ushered him to a world of shadows and dreams. With steady breath and a serene expression, Endymion was carried into Selene's chariot. Winged steeds bore his weight as they made their way to the desolate rock.

Silent and overwhelmed by the unfolding events, Selene, aware of her role as his support and guide to eternal oblivion, shed no tears. Two shepherds were waiting for their arrival; they lifted Endymion and carried him into the magnificent starlit cave. Selene entered, casting her faint silvery light against the starry dome, and departed swiftly, for she had her nightly journey awaiting her.

Later, in the gentle twilight, she returned to the cave her family was calling "Selene's Mausoleum" and found him still, peaceful, on his granite rock bed. Holding his hand, she saw a faint smile grace his face and noticed his eyes flutter. During her visit, when she talked to him, it sometimes made a difference: he would smile, frown, twitch. Yet for the most part, he remained still, his mind impenetrable, his thoughts unreadable.

She longed for the vibrant Endymion of the past and from time to time would see him in her dreams, youthful and vigorous. It was disheartening.

Since that transition, the pale moon had stripped herself of all her customary silver adornments. She took to arriving at the cave at the same hour of the night, often in deep thought, troubled, examining notions of birth and death, life and eternity, mortality and loss. Selene carried the burden of grief and memories of the bittersweet days she had shared with Endymion. It was a period of transition into the unknown, driving her to ponder alternative ways of navigating the gendered patriarchy that governed her world. A secret resentment toward Zeus fueled her determination.

On the night of the first full moon, Selene chose to stay away from the cave. When she met the sun-god at the change of the hours, she confessed, "Dear brother, I felt lost last night, and yet I found solace in solitude."

Helios, a husband, lover, and suitor to many, grinned and winked at his sister. "Take heart. A lover may be lost, but love never is."

Perplexed, Selene ignored his remark with a shrug. "I want to thank Perse for all the help, coordination, and follow-through. You are lucky, Helios. She deserves a gathering place of her own. If she needs any help . . ."

Helios interjected, "She has recruited Daedalus, the man who built Pacifae and Minos's palace in Crete. Don't be surprised if she calls on you soon."

NINETEEN

NEW HOPE FOR A GRIEVING FATHER

*I*n the serene ambience of Perse's garden, under the gazebo, the sisters would occasionally meet for breakfast. Perse loved the fountain with its weathered stone figures and the soothing melodies of bubbling water—though that made no impact when their conversations centered on the tragic story of Daedalus's loss.

Clymene, her voice fervent, complained, "Minos is impervious to feelings and ignores the consequences of his actions. His desires reign supreme. The boy drowned because of him."

Pensive, Perse observed, "The Cretans are ambitious, and certainly my daughter Pacifae—she is enigmatic! I don't understand her infatuation with a bull!" The discordant calls of crows arguing over a crop of berries disrupted the conversation.

"Who can fathom the whims of gods?" Clymene spoke quickly, but then her tenor sharpened, pregnant with a challenge. "How can gods, rulers of earthly realms, the mountains, and the heavens, snatch away our precious children, steal our joy? Phaethon died in the prime of his youth, and so did sweet Icarus."

"I feel your pain, dear sister," Perse sighed. "Helios told me Icarus was a gifted, handsome boy with blue eyes and golden hair . . . a talented athlete."

Clymene frowned. "As good a swimmer as he was, someone wanted him drowned. I cannot imagine his father's agony, watching the boy wrestle with the waves and . . . I had nightmares about it. Where is compassion, where is justice?"

Perse smiled a bitter smile. "I am glad to see you are finally angry, sister. I think of your son's loss and then of Icarus's death, and 'golden ichor' boils in my veins. Immortals have no compassion for humans, using them like harriers to the winds. I think of Troy, a proud city now destroyed. One day it is Zeus's whims and on another day it is King Minos's possessiveness that destroys."

The queen was troubled as she watched her sister reach for a handkerchief. The unsettling conversation and the repeated loud caws of three crows had transported the sisters to a realm of unease and uncertainty about the future.

The prevailing opinion among the members of Helios's court was that Minos's decision to imprison Daedalus and Icarus was harsh, selfish, and undeserved. The royals had been publicly silent, but when Daedalus lost his son, Helios spoke out.

One evening in the torchlit Great Hall, the all-knowing sun-god leaned on his throne, unable to forget that he was an eyewitness to the tragic drowning of Icarus. His shoulders slumped, he cleared his throat and said to his wife, "I lose faith in ungrateful rulers who imprison their subjects because they hold the power of an office, especially when they ought to be grateful to the man. Not only that, our daughter is amid her own controversy. Shame!" It was unusual for him to express his disapproval of Pacifae in public.

Shaking her head, the queen answered, "I usually stay out of their business, but this time . . ."

When Perse proposed it, the usually diplomatic Helios readily agreed to send a scalding message with a homing pigeon.

From the House of Helios
To King Minos and Queen Pacifae,

> To punish an innocent man who solved your problem of housing the dangerous Minotaur is a grave error. A father lost his beloved son, and that has to be attributed to your cruel decision to imprison them. We are placing Master Daedalus under our protection. Be gracious and send him an apology.
> Helios and Perse

No one gossiped like the people of Helios's court, and besides, the royals had made no secret of this message. It was good for court morale for the people to know, as it supported the sun-god's reputation for being fair-minded.

The same day, Perse sent an invitation to Daedalus, after Helios read and readily agreed to it.

The royals of Crete never responded.

The offer came at the right moment. Heartbroken about his son's death, Daedalus was ready to move on when the queen asked him to her palace. He had wrestled with the waves and lifted the boy's lifeless body away from Poseidon's gripping arms to a nearby island, pleading to have him back, for it was cruel for any father to bury his son.

Why not me, if one must be gone, he thought, shedding bitter tears on the sandy beach, laying the boy's still body next to the rock that would become a marker for his resting place. There were times when he pivoted from anger against Minos to sorrow, to blaming himself for escaping from Crete. *My son would*

140

be alive had we stayed. "We should have stayed in Crete," he muttered. That next month, Daedalus endured his pain, calling on his memories, alive but not living fully.

Despite the sorrow and anger he felt toward Helios, the god who had melted his son's wax wings, the allure of the offer tugged at his heart. Caught between grief and the desire for healing, he knew he had to make a decision.

He took a few days to consider her offer, which was delivered by her homing pigeons. It was a generous proposal: under her protection, Perse vowed, he would have all the help, manpower, material, and equipment necessary, and safe passage from Icaria to the palace.

As Daedalus recalled Queen Pacifae's words about her mother's vision, a glimmer of hope sparked within him. The concept of building a gathering place fit to host pacifist gods resonated with his desire to bring about positive change and prevent further bloodshed. The notion of designing a place where gods could come together to advocate for peace, changing the course of history, intrigued him. Pacifae had told him, "Perse is a mighty and capable queen and sticks to her goals. I admire my mother's wish to create a space for those who abhor war and quarrels that lead to death, who satisfy gods that take sides and protect leaders who take arms against each other. I don't know if she can succeed."

He considered it a high compliment to be chosen to oversee the creation of a space intended to become a center for the first council of a pacifist circle. However, skeptical about deceits, Daedalus needed proof that this was a genuine invitation from Queen Perse herself and not a ruse. He thought awhile and then scribbled a simple question on a note he tied to the homing pigeon's back and sent it on its way. Only a few knew the answer he sought, and he believed that Perse would.

It would be an honor. Having faced the guiles of this world, I would accept the offer from the true queen of Helios's palace. I pray you do not take offense, as I send an authentication question: Who is Pacifae's secret son that lives in the labyrinth, and the names of her daughters?

Perse must, he figured, know about the Minotaur, the creature living in Crete that was half man, half bull. An odd beast, he was born to Queen Pacifae, the product of her lying with a bull! An embarrassed King Minos had Daedalus build a labyrinth to hide and lock away the hungry creature. The whole affair did not stay secret for long.

A day later, Daedalus got his answer from the queen. The homing pigeon returned with the short list: Minotaur, Ariadne, Akalli, and Phaedra.

Helios kept his promises to Perse. She was a faithful wife and strong ally. She deserved his support for the building project, and he realized that he could see value in her mission. He tracked Daedalus's ship and placed it under his protection, casting days of good weather and fair winds. The slender vessel traveled smoothly downwind, and the evening before its arrival, the sun-god informed the queen that it was time to send a party to welcome Daedalus at the harbor.

They waited on the jetty for the ship to appear. As it sailed into the bay and dropped anchor, a small group of locals, mostly palace guards, sent out a rowboat that approached the ship to receive the special passenger: a tall, thin man climbing in with few belongings. When the oarsmen landed it on the shoreline, a porter carried what he had brought with him, and the special guest followed the officer and a couple of guards that marched behind them.

Resting for a minute near the top of the terraced hill, Daedalus saw a massive two-story palace with the grand entrance, a complex structure unique to the area by grandeur and style.

Perse had sent Leonora to meet him at the entrance and offer him every accommodation. Her servant led the slender, graying man to his room, located on the palace ground floor. His window faced Mount Olympus, and the furnishings reflected his special standing and importance to his hosts. His bed was raised and comfortable, and there was a wide table, a chair, and a wooden chest in the room. He found a basin and pitcher filled with water and washed, combed his curls, and changed into a plain white tunic. Although tired from the long journey, he followed the lingering Leonora to the garden to meet the queen.

When majestic Perse came into view, he bowed, lowering his eyes to the well-groomed lawn. "My queen, at your service. Thank you for your invitation."

She was dressed in an elegant amber tunic, with a hazel meander running around the hem, flowing sleeves, and a plain golden necklace.

They locked eyes and she sat across from him, examining slowly the evidence of a traveler's fatigue. "Dear Daedalus, welcome to Helios's country. I hope you had a good journey and your accommodations are comfortable."

He bowed again. "I am grateful and reassured that in your world, guests are protected by Xenios Zeus." He remained standing.

She noticed his shoulders slumped as he wiped his forehead dry. Though he seemed sturdy, his smile was that of a weary man as his bright eyes examined the room.

"You live in a majestic palace, my queen, and I thank you for offering me excellent accommodations. I am honored to have the chance to work on a very special project and am grateful for your protection."

He is certainly polite, Perse was thinking. He appeared to listen to her carefully and seemed appreciative to have a significant project, but his words were stilted, formal. In response, she asked, "What news do you bring us from your travels and from my daughter Pacifae?"

At first thoughtful, Daedalus finally gave her a quick update. *I am at her mercy . . . it is best to be honest*, Daedalus thought. After praising the royal family of Crete, he then spoke of the recent developments. "We left Crete just as a battle was about to break out between Minos and the Athenians"—he cleared his throat—"who had killed his son, my queen."

"Another war!"

He could see Perse glower.

"Threatening Athens?"

"Yes, Minos wanted to keep us on his island, though he offered to release Icarus if he agreed to join his army, which needed more men. In our effort to escape from Crete and the threat of another war, I lost my son and realized that I have riled Minos's anger. I am so grateful—delighted—to get your invitation and want to contribute to your mission with all my heart."

"You are safe here, and I am sorry for your loss," Perse said. "I want to provide everything you need so that what we create is a suitable temple of peace. One where immortals would want to gather and contribute to peace for humanity. We, too, have seen a young man, along with our dear boy, Orion, leave for Athens because my husband, during a festive night, promised it, and he always keeps his promises. Such a waste!"

He watched her hide her hands in her pockets, take a deep breath, and continue.

"Deep down, he recognizes we need to give peace a chance. Even more reason to create this space and organize opposition to unnecessary quarrels, bloody battles, and death that feed the jaws of Hades. But you have had a long trip. Let's wait a day or two before we discuss the project. Meanwhile, tell me, what will you need to develop plans?"

He explained that a project of such importance and size would attract specialized quarrymen, carpenters, metalworkers, and stonemasons that he would have to identify among the locals and from other parts of the world once he had drawn final plans. Daedalus concluded, "But first, I want to tour every corner of this amazing palace, fit for the sun-god and his queen. It will help me form proposals that work. It is a good place to start in the next day or so." He saw Perse smile and judged that she seemed pleased to hear him talk about the project.

"I expect no less from you. You are free to search and identify such men; I will pay them well. Let me know what you need as you move along. You can take all the time needed to plan before you show me your proposals. I will assign one of my trusted young men to take care of your needs, run errands, and be available to you while you are here," she said, arranging her necklace on her chest.

He was tired and was trying to ignore the start of a headache by pressing his temples with the heels of his hands.

"I want to introduce you to Helios soon," the queen explained. "Know that he did not intend to harm your son. It was cruel nature taking its course. Relax for a few days, meet people, and explore. We will meet again when you have toured and are rested."

The queen motioned for Leonora to escort him back to his quarters and asked her to introduce Leon, a young slave whom she placed in Daedalus's service day and night. "Rest well!" Perse moved to the staircase leading to her quarters.

TWENTY

GETTING ACQUAINTED

*P*erse sought out Helios when he returned to the stables at sunset. In the soft rosy light of a clear sky, she watched him step off his chariot and hand the reins to Asim, who was ready to collect the team and lead the horses to the arena. The grooms were preparing to give them the care they deserved after another long trek around the globe. Her husband looked so handsome. Her heart quickened as she watched the activity for a minute. The all-seeing sun-god turned when Perse called him, his chest puffing out, and said, "My dear, Daedalus has arrived safe and sound. So, what do you think of him?"

She rushed to his side, reached out, and smoothed his wind-swept curls. Her words flowed effortlessly. "He is older than I expected, a distinguished gentleman with impeccable manners, still mourning the death of his son. Be gentle with him. I assured him you had no intention of harming his son. Icarus overestimated the resilience of his wings."

"The Fates have spoken." He interlocked his arms across his chest. "Death is predestined for young and old. I am sorry for his loss, but I had no malicious intent to harm Icarus. Daedalus will find only compassion from us here."

Perse took his hand, and they walked to the palace side by side.

"How did he strike you?" asked Helios.

"A cautious man, he needed assurances before accepting our invitation, making sure the invitation was coming from this house. I offered him protection from Minos and our daughter Pacifae, who would certainly want him back in Crete. I have guaranteed his safety here." She saw him nod in agreement and continued, "He has asked for access to the entire building, to learn the shape of the palace."

Helios narrowed his eyes. "I can guarantee his safety, but I don't want him lingering in my quarters!"

"Don't worry. I have assigned Leon, my trusted slave, to aid him and keep me informed. He follows instructions. I will ask him to accompany Daedalus when he tours the palace and to stop at your quarters only once, while you are away." Perse knew that on rare occasions Clymene or other partners might occupy his rooms and trusted the boy's discretion.

"I would like to meet him. Invite him to join us in the Great Hall. We will introduce him and make sure people welcome and treat him well."

When they had reached the palace, she gave him a quick peck on his cheek, and they parted, taking the marble stairway to their own quarters.

Although his eyelids were heavy, his churning thoughts would not release him to sleep. In the night's pit, restless, Daedalus tuned into unfamiliar sounds his first few nights at the palace: chirping crickets, a girl's laughter, the yelp of a dog, his servant's breathing. Stretched out on his bed, lightly covered with a linen blanket, the long-legged man watched a sliver of the moon coming through slightly drawn shutters and resting on the floor. He checked on young Leon, sleeping on a floor mat.

The night breeze carried in wafts of sweet smells from the kitchen as acid churned in his stomach. The days when he would chat with young, eager Icarus before falling asleep were gone forever. He missed his boy: Icarus's easy laughter, optimism, risk-taking, and his affectionate ways of still hugging his father. There were days he turned, thinking he heard his son's voice calling, "Papa . . ."—though it was rare anymore. Clymene had lost her son from Helios's seed. The queen said she was sorry for Icarus's death, and others had been sympathetic, but they did not know what it was to see him every day, to watch him grow; he had been an essential companion to his father's days, a reason for being. How could they guess what it was like to know that his dreams, hopes, and ambitions would never come to pass? And then there was Minos, his battles, the nonsensical loss of young lives.

"What good is my fame," he whispered, "when he is not alive to share in my days and enjoy any privilege life would afford us?" The pain was still raw. The only cure he knew was to throw himself into his work and create a monument of peace in his memory.

But how did these goddesses hope to challenge quarreling among gods and humans? If there was a way, even if they could have only minor success, he would dedicate his days to Perse's efforts. Queen Perse had sparkly eyes and a look of determination. Although too early to know, he believed Pacifae was right to call her a willful woman who wielded a great deal of power. How many eons had she been plotting on reaching her goal? She, a lesser goddess, seemed to have a resolve greater than the mighty twelve of Mount Olympus; perhaps her alliances and hard work would bear good results.

He had just met young Leon earlier that evening, a robust, intelligent young man who had worked as a stonemason for one of the palace's projects. Under a mop of black, curly hair, the lad had growing fuzz on his rosy cheeks. His eagerness to please Daedalus was obvious. "So happy to be your servant, Master Daedalus. I am at your service and hope to learn a great deal from you."

Leon reminded him of his son. Daedalus slapped his back and smiled. "You will be my right-hand man. I want you to introduce me to all the craftsmen of our trade who have a good reputation and show me every corner of the palace."

In the faint light of the moon, he checked on the young man again and smiled, hearing his even breathing. Turning to his side, he sighed, felt his eyelids get leaden, and let the relief of heavy darkness envelop his mind.

By the end of his first week, Daedalus had mapped the shape of this elaborate palace, following Leon around the two-story structure, starting with the basement. He toured the dimly lit rooms and saw a well-stocked assortment of clay amphorae that stood tall with broad bases and narrow necks. Some contained fine oils, collected from the bountiful palace groves. Others were filled with fine wines imported from nearby islands. In other rooms were marble statues, alabaster jars, pottery, and decorative items stored in boxes for use on special occasions. Some pots were utilitarian, containing grains, olives, cheese, and pulses, while others, delicate and ornate, were meant to hold cosmetics or perfume.

The first floor was impressive. It unfolded as a tapestry of opulence and functionality. From the bustling kitchen to the tranquil gardens, the grand hall to the entertainment spaces for the courtesans, this floor offered a glimpse into the vibrant world of the palace. Nestled in a corner, the out-of-the-way kitchen hummed with constant activity. Next to the well-manicured gardens stood the Great Hall, the heart of the palace social gatherings, adorned with columns, elaborate tapestries, and intricate mosaics that depicted Helios in glory. Smaller, finely decorated rooms were available for conversation and games.

A grand staircase led to the second floor, where the private quarters of the royals were laid out to offer the utmost comfort and grandeur. With magnificent views of Mount Olympus, large windows, and multiple rooms for the residents, they were the private sanctuaries for Helios and his family. Only trusted servants were allowed on this floor to look after the royals.

Daedalus studied the building complex and found it sound; it was laced with impressive interior and exterior staircases, light wells, massive columns, and lovely gardens. He had to be sure, but it looked as if the structure could support a third floor.

Helios's quarters were well lit, roomy, and airy, with views. They were decorated with art, mosaics, and paintings that gave the visitor a sense of glory and power. It was obvious that the sun-god was a self-centered essential force of nature whose dedication to ruling the day earned him favors from the Olympians. He *had* to be self-centered, like most immortals, but how did he use his status? Daedalus anticipated meeting Helios—his son's inadvertent destroyer—with fear and trepidation in his heart. He looked forward to getting to know Clymene, who was still grieving, Leon had told him, as was he. As for Perse, she exuded energy, and he already considered her an important ally, essential to the success of the project.

When Perse summoned him to the Great Hall one evening to meet Helios and be his honored guest, the master architect found himself filled with anticipation, curiosity, and some reluctance. Eager to make a favorable impression, he asked trusted Leon about the dress and customs of the court. The youth hastened to consult Leonora, who offered this advice: "It is best to be modest and humble in his presence. Keep a simple attire and a respectful manner. The queen will be there to assure a successful introduction."

In an understated yet refined ensemble, he arrived at the crowded Great Hall with an air of quiet confidence. The bright notes of a salpinx announced his arrival, and the sight of brilliant Helios dazzled him. The sun-god was resting on his throne in fine purple robes, wearing a crown of sunrays over his thick blond hair. Graceful Perse sat next to him in a crimson silk robe belted with a golden chain, and she was talking to Clymene, who met the newcomer in plain black robes and a lacy headdress.

Daedalus made eye contact with the queen, who gestured, inviting him to approach the royals. It was not his first time visiting the hall, but this time it was crowded with palace courtesans, guards, priests, and busy servants, dressed in their finery and curious to meet the famous architect.

It was an unusual reception for a mere mortal, and when he walked into the large hall with the massive columns, he took a low bow as soon as he oriented to the sun-god. Sitting on his throne, Helios was breathtaking, shimmering, yet friendly in a way that made him less intimidating.

Daedalus addressed the royals as he approached, "It is my good fortune and delight to serve life-giving Helios, the ruler of daylight and the seasons, his queen, Perse, and all those in this house."

Helios inclined his head approvingly and motioned for a servant girl to pour his guest wine. Once Daedalus was served, the sun-god raised his golden cylix and called out to the crowd: "In the year to come, we have the honor to host Master Daedalus, the gifted creator of Minos and our daughter Pacifae's palace. He is my honored guest and will have free access to the palace.

Welcome him whenever you see him. He is here to design a space fit for gathering immortals my queen will host. If you can assist him in this project, don't hesitate to let him know."

Everyone raised their cylices and took a sip of wine, wishing Daedalus a pleasant stay and success in his project. The lead of the palace guards, wearing a helmet crested with sunrays, approached him and offered him the aid of his men, should he require it. The foundry master, a dark-skinned Ethiopian, introduced himself and handed Daedalus samples of dice made of stone—marble, lapis, and carnelian—inviting him to tour the sites he managed. Then he introduced his daughter, a middle-aged woman with a trim waistline and elaborate hairdo; she was an artist who had produced paintings featuring Helios in and around the palace. Daedalus asked their names, shook hands, and promised to meet them soon and learn more about what they offered.

Perse moved easily into the crowd and, taking the master by his hand, led him to Helios, who was conversing with Clymene. The sun-god stepped down from his throne and said, "Welcome, Daedalus. I hope your trip was safe and your quarters are comfortable. What do you think of the palace?"

Grateful for the small talk, the architect responded, "Thank you for the hospitality. All is well. It is enormous, this palace with one thousand rooms, and it has a solid structure. It is a beautiful building with multiple stories that inspire with its large, well-lit rooms and many staircases. I hope to please you by designing a new space worthy of you and those you will host."

"Yes, two floors and a basement we use for storage, a small temple dedicated to Olympian gods, gardens, stables, and smaller buildings around the estate. An adequate abode," said Helios. Hesitating, and after checking with Perse who nodded encouragingly, he continued, ". . . although my son's quarters will remain forever empty. We share the loss of our precious boys. I am sorry about Icarus's demise; I did not intend it. Too late I thought to hide behind the clouds to protect him."

Daedalus stiffened and looked over at Clymene, whom he had come across before this gathering. He had learned from Leon that she had recently lost her son, fathered by Helios. He drifted into thoughts unspoken until that moment. "It is not possible to fill the empty space. I miss my only son. What sustains me today is my work and the purpose of this project. I will pour all my heart into creating a sanctuary for peace and the gods that support it. It almost feels like a monument to their young souls, lost before their time."

The spirit of Daedalus's words opened the royal hearts. Helios slipped his hand into Clymene's and smiled. His voice was soft and warm. "Today we are celebrating your arrival, Master Daedalus. Tomorrow you can tell us what you need, and you shall have it. I know Perse will attend to your needs. She is eager to start and will meet with you in the morning."

And so it was that the ice thawed and Daedalus bowed to the royals, grateful to be in a safe place, away from angry Minos and Pacifae and supporting Perse's goal, one he shared. He hoped that he would create a worthy place to meet that would unleash the spirit of peace and healing forces for the world.

TWENTY-ONE

NEW LOSS
AS PLANNING BEGINS

When Melpomene arrived to help her mistress dress for the breakfast meeting with Perse and Daedalus, Clymene couldn't help but notice she was not carrying any clothes or shoes. Her servant seemed eager to share the morning news. Curious and with some growing unease, Clymene inquired, "So, what do you know?"

Melpomene's expression turned solemn as she delivered the devastating news: "Sailors from Athens brought home Orion's body yesterday; he died in battle outside Athens, my mistress. I am deeply sorry to bring you such heartbreaking news."

Clymene took a long, agonizing breath, unable to find words. When the maid handed her a pair of earrings, the nereid motioned them away, whimpering. She sat on her bench and when she could finally speak, she challenged her servant, "It's not possible. He just left us for Athens. Where did you hear such nonsense?" *No more deaths*, she thought as the sadness of Phaethon's loss stormed inside her unchecked.

Melpomene rearranged a couple of pillows silently and waited for her mistress's orders.

"Please, fetch me some suitable attire and my lapis necklace."

When her maid returned, Clymene's demeanor had shifted, her previous turmoil now contained with a façade of composure. She carefully selected the plain black tunic with a streak of raindrops painted on the skirt, let her hair loose on her shoulders, and tucked an embroidered handkerchief into her pocket. Melpomene approached her mistress, deftly securing the lapis necklace, and extended a small mirror, offering Clymene a moment longer to compose herself.

"I cannot bear such news. Where did you hear that?" she asked again.

The girl answered in a calm, steady voice, "It's true, my lady. I saw the men carrying his body to his family home. It devastated his only brother, who received them."

Clymene's voice resonated with chagrin. "Circe and I warned him. We all did and tried to dissuade him. Restless youth!" The impact of the news brought more tears to her eyes. "My son's good friend is gone! So is my Phaethon." She took out her handkerchief, which soon was soaked, and covered her face, refusing the mirror.

"They are waiting for you, mistress," said Melpomene.

Clymene knew she was expected at the gazebo covered with wisteria for a leisurely breakfast. Her sister had planned for them to meet and share ideas about the project.

"Find out for me when they plan his funeral," she ordered, before covering her head with a black scarf and taking the stairs to find the others.

Perse and Daedalus were discussing the terrible news that had struck everyone in the palace like a bolt of lightning. Clymene could see the tall man's shoulders had caved in and his fists were clenched. He had a pained grimace on his face when he spoke. "At least it was a quick death. It's one of the crazy things we wish for ourselves, instead of our loved ones."

As Clymene absorbed the weight of the tragic news, her thoughts drifted to Icarus, imagining his fall as though it were her own son drowning in the unforgiving sea, no doubt an agonizing moment for his father. Listening in, she learned that the battle had cost many Athenian lives. Orion, Phaethon's young friend and companion, had succumbed to a wound that came from an Athenian spear. In that moment of shared grief, Clymene reached out instinctively, gently gripping the man's arm. "Daedalus, I cannot imagine the sorrow of such a loss for your family."

The man cast his deep brown eyes to the distance. "Losing a child is a pain no parent should have to endure. You and I know about such loss, my mistress," he said softly, looking into her eyes.

Covering her heart, she whispered to herself, "All alone, away from loved ones—what a terrible fate for a brave, young soul." Wringing her hands then, she watched the queen, who was pacing around the table, her eyes blazing as she spoke.

"It's a savage world, Clymene. So much unnecessary death. More souls crowding into Hades because of Minos and Pacifae's revenge. Is there no place for reconciliation and forgiveness?"

Perse signaled for Leonora to set the table and her servant brought out milk, bread, honey, cheese, and fresh fruits. They sat down and started filling their dishes and cups as Phaethon's mother declared, "I will not deny that the world is making very little sense to me. Wise leaders look for solutions, compromise. Thoughtless, angry gods and unforgiving mortals cause the loss of so many innocents." She continued with the obvious question: "Why did Helios agree to let his men join Minos's army?"

The hostility in her tone surprised Perse, who, despite her own convictions, attempted an explanation. "Remember the celebration at the end of the olive harvest? He was so pleased with the rich crops and the crews' hard work that he was willing to grant any favors. One wanted to be released from this house and join Minos's army. That opened the gates for trouble. He could not deny those who asked to follow him." The queen left the table and soon returned, holding an olive branch. She set it on the table. "One curse of the past is its inevitability. We cannot undo it, change events, and restore life. All we can do is learn and be watchful so that it does not happen again. That is my purpose and mission, to seek peaceful solutions and avert wars."

"I worry about Helios. We need to hear that he will support us and join in," said Clymene, reaching for some fresh fruit, "but you can count on me, dear sister, for any support I can give to this cause."

"I am honored to partake," Daedalus piped in. "I willingly join you in building this space that will host like-minded gods and goddesses, my royal ladies."

"Presently, our only course is to focus on creating a space for peace," Perse continued, clearly on a roll. "A physical space, a setting that is safe and calm, that invites and encourages efforts that would lead to helpful interventions. The task is arduous. We will need all the support we can muster because there are potent forces against us. Let's focus on creating such a place. Daedalus, can you lead us in a brainstorm that would help conceptualize the space for this project?"

Daedalus spoke gravely, and the women listened attentively. "It has to be extraordinary, a site that invites, offers serenity, and suggests open communication, setting a tone of harmony and synchronicity. It should be a place that offers an aesthetically pleasing, tranquil environment to those who gather to identify peaceful solutions for the common good. I hope you agree that what we need in times of crisis are open conversations, negotiation, forgiveness, and peaceful resolutions."

Perse's foot tapped impatiently. Smiling politely, she interrupted him. "Master Daedalus, I am delighted that you see what we are trying to accomplish. How can we assist you as you start your planning?"

He quickly swallowed a bite of cheese and offered, "Location is one element we need to sort out. The palace is a multilevel structure, two stories above ground. We can consider building a new extension off the ground floor with a view of the mountain and possibly including restful plantings and water features. But you must have ideas of your own to share, so please give us your top choices."

The moment was finally here to push forward ideas that had been incubating. Barely interested in others' opinions, the queen wanted the space to be grand and easily accessible. It could be an interior remodel or an outdoor extension of the palace. An animated Perse gestured broadly in the mountain's direction, voicing one option. "Another approach would be to renovate and open existing rooms that face Mount Olympus and join them to build a large columned hall that is decorated with symbols of peace. After all, this is the palace with one thousand rooms. I like the idea of including plants and water features."

Next, it was Clymene's turn. She had walked out into the garden and was pointing to the second floor. "Would it be possible to build a third floor that opens to the sky, with or without a roof? It could connect to the ground floor if we extended the grand staircase. Does the current structure support such an undertaking?" She looked at Daedalus.

He nodded. "A very creative and ambitious idea, my lady! These three thoughts are a good place to start." He picked up the olive branch. "This can become a decorative leitmotif that could appear on benches, fountains, columns, and other spots. It all is possible; each approach presents distinct challenges, all manageable. Shall we consider other options or work with these three main ideas?"

Predictably, Perse's impatience dictated her answer. Still tapping her foot, she filled her cup with milk and, setting the decanter down, confirmed: "Three are enough. I think this is a good place to start. We should approach Hecate and Selene, reach out to Demeter and Hera, and have them identify what they prefer. Could you sketch out representations of each to use when we solicit preferences?"

Gently, ever-observant Clymene interrupted. "Each time you bring up this notion, you seem to narrow support for peace to female goddesses, my dear Perse. For one, Helios is very much a part of this project. I would like to see us engage other male gods, as I believe there are several who would support peace! But first of all, Helios. Daedalus, although not immortal, is a model of a man who understands and sees value in this effort. Why not gain more allies and strengthen our core of support? Thus, the all-seeing Helios would have the company of other gods and would be enthusiastic to join us."

Perse forced a smile. "Your thought has merit, Clymene. Could you test it out? Would you like to do some outreach?"

"I will, starting with Helios, who knows all. He would have suggestions that would help us. But I also think that he should be the one to choose the location. After all, this is his palace!"

Perse noticed that Clymene was watching her. *Does she imagine that her words might awaken a twinge of jealousy in me? He is, after all, my husband and often consults with me in making decisions.* "You have always preferred being transparent with your thoughts, my sister."

The discussion continued well past noon; the table had been cleared and after a lot of debate Clymene's suggestion of a third floor ended up appealing to all three. They reasoned that living mostly on the rugged slopes of Olympus, the important future congregants would appreciate reminders of green hills and valleys of Mother Earth. "A space that softens the craggy mountain terrain is a desirable direction and is viable," said Daedalus, and a wide grin lit his face. "It could be an open structure built on terraces with plants and trees growing on them. A complicated irrigation system would allow for a lush and verdant environment, either with a ceiling supported by columns or open to the sky, or some of each."

In the end, the three agreed to present to Helios sketches of all three options and seek his open endorsement. Over the morning's conversation, Perse became aware yet again of the variety of skills and specialized knowledge that would be required to carry out such an ambitious, complex concept. She understood that Daedalus would have to design and oversee the construction, and potentially map a water and irrigation system to sustain plants and trees in the gardens. He would also need stonemasons to cut and shape the stones that would compose the third level, a place to meet, terraces, and other structural elements on the site.

Daedalus proceeded to educate them about the range of expert capabilities required to undertake this project. He spoke about recruiting carpenters to build wooden frameworks and supports needed to hold up new floors and plumbers and gardeners who would select plants and arrange them in an aesthetically pleasing fashion. Perse reminded him that he had access to the palace guard to carry out some of the labor; however, he was welcome to recruit people he needed and crew masters that would help him run the operation. It was a good session that left each of them excited and overwhelmed by the scope of this project.

There was more to attend to during the day. Wrapping up the meeting, Perse turned to Daedalus with new respect and asked him, "I have one last question, Master Daedalus. What do you need to start your work at this point?"

"Thank you for asking, my queen. I need to have the use of a well-lit room with a large drawing table to meet with crafts-men, draw and lay out plans, and give them instructions as we develop final plans. It would be a place to meet with you and Helios Hyperion, to get your approvals, report developments and any problems that come up, and track progress. And of course, I need to recruit more skilled workers for some tasks. There are some people I have trained who could help move this project forward. They are in Crete and worked with me to build Minos's palace. Is it possible to bring them here if they agree to come and help us?"

"Give us their names and where to find them. I will send my people to bring them back if they would like to work with you again. They will have lodgings and food and will be rewarded if they agree. I think it would help if you wrote out job offers."

Daedalus ran his hand through his gray hair. "Of course! It will make a vast difference, my queen. Thank you." He walked away after taking a slight bow toward the ladies.

With that, Clymene bade Perse good day and left for her study to begin her own list of potential allies. Perse thought of enlisting their ambassador and his people in Crete to expedite the outreach. They had accomplished a lot. Gleefully, she strut-ted to her quarters, pleased with the progress, and decided she would have Leonora prepare her bath to help her relax from the intense morning session.

TWENTY–TWO

DRAWINGS AND
OUTREACH FOR PEACE

*A*fter the meeting, Daedalus sprang to his feet and asked him to inspect the roof, check its soundness, and identify the direction of the mountain. Leon guided him up the grand staircase to the second floor, leading him to a cramped closet next to Helios's quarters. The space was dark and dank, but a sturdy ladder offered access to the roof. The steps were sound, and he climbed, removed the hatch, and lifted himself outside into the bright daylight and the clear blue sky.

Miraculously, Helios was shining right above the palace. Was he smiling? It was difficult for the architect to say, as his eyes blotched bright circles and spots, and he smiled back blindly. This new sun-master overwhelmed and dazzled him. *Clymene was right. It is important to know he is behind the project.* Looking at the wide expanse, he marveled and asked Leon, "On a clear day like today, a new structure on the roof would be glorious, don't you think?"

"I have never been on the roof before. The view is astonishing," the young man agreed. "But the foundation to support another level would need to be reinforced, Master

Daedalus—exciting and challenging. I cannot wait to see your plan."

"Lady Clymene's idea is the best suited and most complex to execute. Assuring a sound structure is our first challenge. It will take extra time. And yet I hope Helios selects it."

He handed Leon a string that he started unraveling and sent him to the far end of the roof facing the lofty Mount Olympus. "Just a rough idea of this dimension," he murmured, and tied a knot where he held it. "It is ample space to impress." He cut the thread with his teeth, and as soon as Leon released his end, he wrapped it around the palm of his hand and put it in his pocket. "Walk around the perimeter of the roof," he called out, "and let me know of any areas that are soft or unstable. I will check them, after you do." Taking a moment to kneel, he settled down, dangled his long legs over a decorative metope adorned with reliefs depicting Helios, Eos, and Selene, and waited.

"It's all solid, master, but not strong enough to support another layer."

The old man smiled, aiming to encourage the youth to continue offering opinions and pleased that this seemed to be a well-maintained structure. He sent Leon away and lingered on the roof. His mortal eyes could not see the throne of Zeus nor the other mighty ones loitering, but the majestic lines of the peaks rising above a belt of low clouds were plenty to enthrall him.

When he returned to the palace, Leon informed him the royal women were back from Orion's funeral. Perse had sent an invitation for him to join them the next morning and present the options to the sun-god. Daedalus had been of two minds about attending the ceremony of burning Orion's body on the pyre; it would bring back painful memories of Icarus. It was the Moirai's fault. They had spun the boys' untimely deaths. Lachesis was the one who seeded the passion for war arts in

Orion and Phaethon's disregard for the counsel of his father and Asim. And then Atropos, the cruelest of them all, had snipped the thread of their lives short. Besides, death had no boundaries, indiscriminately reaping mortals and demigods alike. Perse's invitation had given him a new purpose. Truthfully, Daedalus felt both relief and guilt about missing Orion's funeral.

He also realized that he had little time to sketch out three proposals. Leon had found paper and sketching implements, and had set a table in their room within a brief time. Over the evening hours and all that night, in the torchlight Leon kept fueled, he worked. In the small hours of the morning, he chose the best three sets for viewing by Helios, Perse, and Clymene and rushed to meet them in a sitting room in Helios's private quarters.

When the sisters walked to the sun-god's quarters they found Daedalus already there. The room had an aura of warmth, bathed in golden hues. It was adorned with opulent furnishings. The walls were painted in a soft, celestial shade of blue; scenes of sunrise and sunset represented the sun-god's journey across the sky. The floor boasted intricate mosaics, with depictions of celestial bodies and constellations. The sisters sat down on comfortable chairs upholstered in rich golden fabrics.

When Helios arrived, he invited them to gather around the gilded table, where Daedalus had placed his sketches. Grinning broadly, he greeted the master with, "What were you doing on the rooftop, Daedalus?" It was the perfect segue to this presentation.

"Exploring the plan that your ladies favor, my lord," he said, spreading out his sets of drawings for them to examine.

Helios peered at them and shuffled them around, asking questions. Finally, he asked, "Tell me what your process will be."

"Your majesty, building this palace extension will require the utmost skilled workforce, dedication, and attention to detail.

My team and I will work tirelessly to create a structure that will stand the test of time and serve as a testament to the greatness of your kingdom and the mission of peace in the world."

An hour later, the three immortals had reached a unanimous decision. The first set of drawings was the most impressive, creating a pleasing and functional space with verdant gardens surrounded by trees. They chose the variation where they would erect a marble amphitheater, partly sunk into the garden in the center of the terraced beds, for gatherings.

Helios was enthusiastic about endorsing the project. "No one has ever seen hanging gardens surrounding an amphitheater on a roof with a view of Mount Olympus," he bragged. It had been Perse's project, really, but he was ready to lend his full support. In his soul, he recognized it was time to take a stance and declare his mission support before he left the group. "The sun will shine brighter over a peaceful world."

The others nodded, and Perse reached out and kissed him lightly on the cheek.

As he started to leave, the urgency of his steps palpable, he heard Clymene say, "You are all-knowing, my lord, with all you see each day. I would like to hear what other gods you believe would support and take part in our Circle of Peace."

"Let me think. I will give you names tonight," he promised, bade them farewell, and hastened away to ride his celestial chariot and herald the arrival of a new dawn.

Three moons had passed, and by then the master had drawn preliminary plans based on measurements his early hires had taken inside and outside the palace. When the master artisans arrived from Crete, building work could start in earnest.

Daedalus's first challenge was to fortify the weight-bearing pillars without affecting the slim, elegant lines of the palace. He tested some of his ideas, starting with the cellars, where massive supports and thicker structures would be acceptable. On the next two floors, he had planned to add archways and metal inserts, using decorative motifs of peace symbols where the additions were visible. He knew that Perse was pleased. However, it was hard to complete that phase without disturbing the royals with noisy tasks. Work would start each day when Helios left the palace and cease when he returned.

He heard that Clymene had the hardest time with the construction noise interrupting her thoughts and was relieved when she shifted her time in her study to evenings, when work had ceased, drafting words inspired by the peace project, words about struggles, aspirations, and sacrifices of gods and mortals hoping to spread peace. Daedalus sometimes watched her leave the palace and wander down to the olive grove or the port. He found her poems lyrical and could identify with Clymene's thoughts and feelings about loss and recovery. He appreciated the effort she made to inspire and extol the benefits of peace those times when she shared her work with him and Perse.

When he checked with Perse to see how she reacted to the necessary racket his crew was making, she did not seem to mind. He found that she liked to be frequently apprised of what tasks the workers carried out. Daedalus met often with her to let her know about supply needs and ask for her preferences in executing the project. While he was focused on the building challenges, he appreciated that the queen spent most of her time recruiting immortals who might support the cause of peace.

All three immortals were doing outreach to identify those willing to join the effort. Even early on, before the building was finished, Perse approached Hera and found her willing to support the cause. The proud majestic Olympian appeared in Perse's scrying mirror one night in response, wearing her crown and carrying her royal lotus-tipped scepter as she spoke. "I see the ills of war. I have watched battles, smelled the stench of rivers of Greek and Trojan blood that covered the land in and outside Troy, witnessed the demise of honorable Achilles, Patroclus, and Hector, who are unhappy shadows in Hades. Peace is a difficult goal to achieve but worthwhile. I will join and assist you, dear Perse. May Daedalus's peace site become scaffolding for us to build more truces, an oasis for peace."

Perse shared Hera's comments with Clymene, who then reached out to Apollo, a god who Helios believed would readily join in their efforts.

Clymene said to her sister, "In my mind, the mission for peace is mostly about battles and wars, but I hope those who join will also combat revenge and smaller quarrels, where most trouble usually starts."

"It is worthwhile to experience some success," Perse agreed.

"If we could have intervened in Minos's situation before the armies took up arms, maybe there would have been no bloodshed," Clymene said. "I become hopeful when I hear about negotiations between leaders and kings. After all, Merops was a skilled negotiator and with him hope always sprang eternal."

The next morning, both sisters sent homing pigeons with messages or lines of new poetry to some Olympians with invitations to join the Circle of Peace. Deep down, Perse considered her sister's approach futile. *Clymene puts too much faith in the power of words. For me, I expect resistance from those gods who took sides in Troy, but I am the ever-optimistic nereid who will not lose hope.*

TWENTY-THREE

ON MOUNT OLYMPUS

Fall had turned into deep winter, as autumn's embrace had yielded to a frigid chill. On a cloudy evening, stars and torchlight softened the evening, and a cozy fire tended by Hestia, the protector of hearth and home, warmed the immortals who had settled in for the evening. Seated amidst the divine assembly, Hera had poured Artemis ambrosia, which she was sipping from a plain, ceramic cylix. It was a present from Perse, decorated with olive branches on the inside and the words "Peace Circle" on the outside.

As Artemis sipped from the vessel, she began to share the weight of recent events. She had lately ascended from a forest outside Athens. Dressed in a long ivory tunic, she had leaned her empty quiver against a weathered boulder as she took in the horrific sight of young bodies strewn around blood-soiled snow where she had gone to hunt. She cleared the dust of snowflakes from a seat and settled down. "Young men in their peak were lying in their own blood, forest animals feasting on their flesh and vampire bats swooping down. It's not that I am not accustomed to bloodshed and mortality, but this was such a devastating sight, a profound, heartbreaking waste of young lives. I couldn't help but think about their mothers, their hearts burdened by unspeakable loss."

Even in the realm of divinity, the plight of mortal mothers resonated, a testament to the enduring bond of love and the universal grief that transcends the boundaries between gods and mortals. Hera, moved by Artemis's words, draped a lavender woolen shawl over her shoulders, replenished her own cylix, and walked to the edge of a craggy pinnacle to look toward Athens. A blanket of fresh snow covered the peaks of Mount Olympus and the forests outside Athens, hiding the violence of the battle. Still, Hera penetrated the remnants with her powerful vision. "The horror of battlefields has long been revulsive to me; it took little persuasion to join Perse's Circle of Peace. Have you heard about it?" she asked blond, youthful Apollo, her voice loud enough to be heard by the handful of others on-site.

The Olympian queen had been listening to him composing music to words he had received from Clymene. He laid down his lyre and asked, "Have you been hearing about this Circle of Peace too? I have received messages about it from another nymph who lives in Helios's house and sends me poetry lines with words that could be mine. She has inspired me to compose songs."

Hestia, the kind, most gentle of goddesses, chimed in with great interest, "What is this Circle of Peace? Tell us more."

She watched him pick up his lyre again, strum a few chords, and turn toward her. "It's an invitation for those of us who object to wars to ally together and work to end them." He began to sing Clymene's verses in his clear tenor voice:

When hands unite, we find relief,
In ways that bring us close to peace.
So let us form a circle round,
And greet the peace that we have found!

CIRCLE OF PEACE

When hands entwine a solace born
Through unity, true peace is sworn.
Together, let us form a sacred ring,
Embracing peace that love will bring.

Apollo's voice resonated through the night air, each word laced with the power to ignite hope. "I want my divine message to inspire all who yearn for an end to conflict to step forward and join the Circle of Peace," he said. The soft, inspiring melody was picked up by a gust of evening breezes that carried it down to the valley, spreading the message over mortals in their sleeping households.

Hera smiled and then turned to answer Hestia. "It's a new effort that comes from the palace of Helios, a much-needed initiative that Perse and Clymene, two Oceanid nymphs, are spearheading with the sun-god, and I fully support. The ravages of the Trojan War and the current battle of Minos's army in Athens have filled land and sky with the gasps and moans of the dying. Their battles divide us, as well, when we decide to protect one mortal camp over another. I invite you to join the Circle of Peace and stop the flames of war, dear Hestia. We need no salpinges to announce it, for those signal wars."

"I have longed for peace for a long time," Hestia answered earnestly, folding her arms across her chest. "Count me in."

Hera nodded and set her scepter on the side of her throne. "Soon there will be a lovely place that Daedalus is building for us to meet, strategize, and take action. It will take more than one of us to make a difference. A gathering of a mighty group would stand a chance to combat this peril that looms among mortals. And we can start today, dealing with Minos's troubles." She took a long breath, hoping that Zeus, who was not engaged, would take a stance, but he offered no words. Then she turned toward Ares, the muscular, youthful god of war who was staring at his father. She could tell he was preparing to protest when he laid down his sharp spear and finely crafted bronze shield and stood up.

Was Ares shivering? She was not sure, but his voice was defiant. "Naive talk! Differences must be resolved with a decisive winner. The best prepared, those possessing excellent strategies and training, should rightfully claim the spoils of victory. I am the god who forges heroes. That is why people love me!"

Athena interjected with a sardonic smile playing upon her lips, "Not so! That is why temples dedicated to you are so scarce!" Her biting words pierced the air.

Hera wondered why Ares should appear surprised, but she also knew that he must see this effort as a clear affront to his reign. Ignoring him, she moved next to Zeus and said, "Hope is one of the most powerful tools we have at our disposal. We will not turn things around in every instance. In fact, our successes may be tiny, but with time, we may learn and improve, stop warring parties from shedding blood." She tilted her scepter in Ares's direction and watched his face changing colors and his fists clench as she said, "Even Ares can help us identify parties before they engage in war. Can't you see the value in such efforts?"

Ares flared back, "I see Apollo composing lovely music, divine and soft and solving nothing. I see Athena with her wisecracks, grandstanding, while I try to help Minos teach a lesson to the Athenians. Remember, out of jealousy they killed his son, who had won amazing victories in competitions. Should I leave the killers unpunished? That is not justice!"

To Hera, Apollo murmured, "He will defy you, but he will not insult you, for you are the wise wife/sister of Zeus. I am with you." He strummed his lyre, picking up the tempo to a new song.

Hera expected a powerful reaction from temperamental Ares. She watched him pick up his weapons, purse his lips tight, and, like an arrow, lift off the edge of a cliff rising above the mountain. He rushed toward Athens as a young, rosy dawn painted the horizon orange. She knew him well enough to expect this explosion of energy and told Apollo, "He has gone to Athens not to hand victory but to continue the bloodbath. We should intervene with Minos and Pacifae to stop it."

"I will send a dream to Minos and Aegeus of Athens that will lead them to negotiate. Blood will spread on their hands and cover their chests. Images of hands reaching out for them in Hades will bring them to the table," answered Apollo.

It was only the beginning, and Ares would resist, but the circle was starting to form. Perhaps it signaled a new dawn.

Zeus, though, was less certain. Would it work out? And was this interference in mortal lives worth the gods' time? What was his often-irritating wife/sister Hera agitating about? Was she trying to get him involved too? He took his drink of ambrosia and settled on a boulder away from the others in the company of eagles that crowded near him. The conversation had him pondering the cost of wars and their benefits. He shifted and interlaced his fingers, resting them on his chest. He frowned, feeling uncomfortable because he hated to betray Ares, his son, who was unpopular to begin with among most gods and mortals, but at the time, Zeus had seen the need to reduce the population of a crowded earth. The loss of life during the Trojan War had pleased him.

This Peace Circle idea was new thought. Should he even consider it? What would his own father, Cronus, do in view of this new movement among his own circle? He mostly did not like to remember him, their struggles, and his demise by Zeus's own hands, but still valued his point of view.

When Athena approached him, adorned in regal attire, he made room for her to sit by him. She exuded an aura of wisdom and grace, and her piercing blue eyes were filled with compassion. Tall and gentle, she took his hand in hers and asked him with the confidence of a favored child, "What do you think about this Peace Circle, Father?"

He counted on her for meaningful exchanges, for she often had a sense of what he was preoccupied with and offered helpful suggestions. "I was going to ask your opinion, as you are the goddess of war and wisdom. What approach should I choose to take, Athena? Would you endeavor to support peace or encourage wars that resolve disputes?"

Athena grounded the conversation in the aftermath of the Trojan War. "I supported the Greeks and helped Odysseus, while you favored the Trojans. When I think about that, I see that taking a position divides us when we meddle in the affairs of mortals. Perhaps we should leave them to their own devices?"

"What made you favor Odysseus, my daughter, and not Agamemnon or Achilles or someone else?" he asked.

She tilted her head thoughtfully and looked toward the dim sunlight on the horizon. "It's difficult to settle that question, Father. What I know is that I favored the Greek king of Ithaca because I appreciated his gift at tactics and spinning yarn. He appeals to me, for he is known among gods and men for his wisdom and cunning. But in the end, he felt abandoned!"

It was a sore topic for Zeus. "Mortals shamelessly blame gods. From us alone, they say, come all their miseries, but they themselves, with their own reckless ways, compound their pains beyond their proper share. As for me, I did support mostly the Trojans. Is there merit to our taking sides?" He stroked his beard and smiled, knowing it would take him time to sort out his stance. "I want to poll more opinions from those who care for the question, and those who have seen more wars than I have."

He noticed his daughter's softening features as she stroked his hand, rising to offer, "You banished your own father, Cronus, to the underworld, but in his day, he saw many more battles among Titans, gods, and mortals. Is he someone to talk to?"

The memory of his father would spring up in moments of difficult decision-making, an uncomfortable memory. He had struggled with Cronus, killed him, and replaced him, creating a new generation of gods and world order. But that old generation was where his roots were. He wondered if it was worth the effort. When his father ruled, he intervened in battles. If he was in charge today, he could impose solutions on Aegeus and Minos. He could even stop action and change the course of events. Traversing time and learning from the past were powers Zeus had not tried to exercise.

In her study, Clymene scribed words that flew off her feathered quill effortlessly. On the long white nights of cold weather and snow, she had shed the hibernation and undertow of winter, already filling pages in her slanted handwriting. It was not her usual experience of writing, rewriting, editing, and reviewing each line over again.

It only happened with poetry she intended to dispatch to the divine and youthful god Apollo. She received, absorbed, and reflected an inner and outer world that was not her own. Was this a fickle thought? She had to trust her intuition, record her inspirations, and, in her best calligraphy, copy the words onto parchment. Each time Clymene read them, she wondered if they were her own or if this was an inspiration directed from above, an echo from another entity. It was exhilarating, overwhelming, even a little scary.

That night, a youthful Apollo appeared in a lucid dream strumming his lyre. He was singing a melodic tune she had never heard before. It was divine. He played it twice. When he repeated the refrain, Clymene realized the lyrics were words she had sent him with her homing pigeons—to greet the dawn of peace!

Her heart was full. She woke up elated and rushed to her writing table, checking the open window for signs and spirits, an old habit that her mother, Tethys, had taught her. Clymene felt a gust of wind rushing into the room, signaling Apollo's presence.

He was spreading seeds of their message over mortals already. *It may take years to germinate*, she thought. Still, she felt a tingling inside her breast. It was all good. He *had* spoken to her; his divine breath was enfolding her with inspiration and a circle of protection. She steadied her hand, dipped the quill into the ink, and wrote new lines.

TWENTY–FOUR

DEBATES

Work continued through sun, rain, and snow, and the building progressed steadily. By spring, the third level was near completion and readily visible above the old roof; it was the legacy of Master Daedalus and the skilled, seasoned managers hailing from the island of Crete.

The owner of the foundry had introduced the master to places where he could purchase materials and had arranged transportation to the construction site. Local shopkeepers had assisted Daedalus in selecting the best materials—marble, limestone, wood, and clay—all then expertly installed. Once the fundamental structure for the third level was finished and planting beds built, expert gardeners planted olive trees, seeding and meticulously transplanting colorful and exotic bushes and ground cover in irrigated terraces.

Daedalus's semicircular amphitheater, with its tiered seating and sunken pit, had already earned him many compliments from early visitors. Made with local stones and fine marble, it was large enough to hold five thousand and grand enough to please auspicious guests; the space boasted unparalleled acoustics. The master had positioned the new structure in such a way as to optimize how the winds would carry sound waves in the amphitheater. During the final stages and without fail, Helios, Perse, and Clymene visited the construction site to watch the progress and offer final guidance to the master.

Clymene and Perse were relentless in campaigning and reaching out to potential recruits through a flurry of messages. Hopeful Perse had assumed that in the day's pantheon, there surely would be many immortals willing to be guardians of peace. Several were sympathetic to her cause but, she feared, would be unwilling to commit. In light of this, and looking for time to strategize, the sisters took to meeting in Perse's weaving room most mornings and working diligently side by side on the loom, encouraging each other and trading news and updates. They had set out to craft a veil for Hera, using several bolts of saffron-colored silk thread, intricately dyed, to surprise and thank her.

Both now realized that the Circle of Peace was not a simple mission. For one awful moment, Perse wanted to give up. "Deaf ears! Can't they see the error of their ways? Poseidon, Hermes, and Hephaestus will not even respond to my calls and invitations." Her mouth had closed tightly against the words.

Once she had regained her focus, working silently on the loom, she asked Clymene, "Have you noticed that there is no god among us dedicated to peace, to calmness, to countering Ares? I could find no one! Have you?" she exclaimed, waving her hands in the air, frustrated as she left the loom.

"It's harder than I thought it would be," Clymene admitted. "After their polite 'good idea' comments, they often avoid us and fade away. Still, they are curious about the gathering place. They would come to see Daedalus's creation. Don't give up, dear sister!"

"We have to petition Zeus to install a god or, better yet, a goddess devoted to peace. We need him to dedicate someone. I promise to pray to her and offer her libations, and so will all mortals." Perse stormed on for a while, finally leaving the room to visit the new gardens that were slowly budding, getting ready for spring. *At least*, she thought, *Daedalus is making good progress.*

In the late hours of the night, well past midnight, as the queen was drifting to sleep, she sensed an unusual surge of energy resonating through her scrying mirror. Perse reached for it to find Hecate revealed. Unexpectedly, the divine sorceress had come with a warning. "I have heard rumors that Ares is organizing resistance. He will not give up easily. Do not become complacent because of a good start, dear Perse. We must remain alert," she advised. "I am joining the Circle because I, too, have lost one of my beloveds in a senseless battle."

There was a loud knock on Ares's door. His daughter Eris, the goddess of unrest, barged into the room, pushing in the door without waiting. "I did not realize they would be so determined in their rabble-rousing and they have some gods joining them," she started. "We have to take action, put a stop to their plans; it would be best if we surprised them."

"Tell me what you know," Ares ordered, aggravated, for she was interrupting his slumber and seemed incoherent.

"They are intervening in Athens and Crete, trying to have the parties start negotiations. We had a protracted war going between them. All was going so swimmingly." Her eyes were wide open and her expression was pained.

"Who are *they?*" he probed, knowing that his daughter sometimes got overexcited. "And how?"

"It started with Hera and Apollo, but now Hestia is joining and . . ."

"Breath in, now out. You talk too fast." He realized he needed to help her restore a sense of calm. Who, after all, could glean information from among all this panic? "You need to slow down."

Still she gulped, wringing her hands. "They are paying visits to the kings of Crete and Athens to force them to work on a truce."

"Where did you hear that?"

"King Minos said it when he was arguing with Pacifae. I was there to add fuel to the fire when Minos blurted it out."

Her words captured his undivided attention. "I will pay a visit to Minos's palace right now," he reassured her, motioning for her to leave. Even before she left the room, he had turned invisible, preparing for his imminent journey.

Quick like a fierce wind, he flew into the Cretan palace throne room, a place he appreciated for its grandeur. It was a richly decorated space with murals punctuated with resting griffins against a burgundy background. No courtiers were present, the benches were empty, but the royal couple filled the space, dressed in their ceremonial clothes. There was a distinct fragrance in the room, something between musk and must, reminding him that Pacifae, the daughter of Helios and Perse, was a well-known sorceress. Invisible, Ares found Minos still arguing with her, loud enough to be heard by the servants. She was sitting on her alabaster throne, fanning herself, and he was pacing furiously.

Disturbing the silence, Minos's anger rang loud. He was waving his arms in the air. "Your son—and I am talking about the Minotaur . . ." He rarely named the beast. "His mere existence is not only embarrassing but is causing me to risk past, important alliances with the Athenians that I cannot afford to lose."

Does he despise her? Ares wondered. *His frown and pursed lips are signs.*

Minos continued, "Your other son, the victor in their games, turned out to be such a braggart; they took his life out of resentment! What is the matter with your children, Pacifae?

They copy your strange choices and warped ways of living and loving!"

Pacifae answered, "It suits you to forget your part, my dear Minos, the part of a father who neglects his wife and children, a husband so unapproachable, even your closest advisors fear you. You have no soft spot for anyone, and you are a coward." She stood up and stopped fanning herself.

"So, I will bring more Athenians here," he went on. "Their bodies will feed the bull. I will honor our son's memory; he has to be avenged for his untimely death, though he appears in my dreams and wants me to end this war. I have to show our pride! You put me in an impossible position."

It is evident that Eris has been at work, thought Ares.

"You love to blame me! My son won't starve. There is plenty of game to hunt." With regal grace, Pacifae moved toward the door. "It has gone on too long. I should negotiate a truce, my beloved, if you can't," she said, turning her back to the king and storming out of the hall.

Ares returned to Mount Olympus, where the word was that Helios's palace was getting closer to welcoming the Peace Circle. Invitations had been sent for an opening ceremony next month. Some Olympians were stopping by the site and pledging their support to Hera. Annoyed and aware, Ares sent his messengers, a pair of vultures always standing by, to invite a council of his helpers. The birds crowed with excitement and leaped into the sky, looking for Phobos (fear), his twin Deimos (violence), and their sister Eris (unrest), faithful allies who had aided Ares in terrifying the world with arguments that led to bloodshed.

They met in the barren fields of Troy, outside the city walls, a land soaked in blood, where Ares had set up a table with four chairs inside an abandoned tent.

The god of war had set his weapons on the floor and waited for the arrivals, reminiscing about Achilles's lust for Hector's blood on the battlefield of Troy. He could remember every detail of the moment he speared Hector, the prince of Troy, in his throat and dragged his corpse behind his chariot. Achilles was the clear winner that day. He admired both warriors; they were worthy, brave, and untamed. Their last fight was glorious; the story was sung into the ages by the famous bard, Homer.

One by one his guests arrived, trickling into the tent, ending his reverie. They saluted each other, raising the right arm from the shoulder into the air, their hands straightened, and called out, "Hail Ares," and he responded the same way.

Before even letting them sit down, Ares spoke with urgency about the purpose of the meeting. "There is an actual threat ahead of us. Helios, his women, and some Olympians are organizing to get rid of us, but I know they cannot accomplish that, not if we put our minds to foil them. This 'Circle of Peace' is right now attempting to intervene, trying to have the king of Athens negotiate with the king of Crete to stop this protracted war.

"Not all Olympians have sided with this movement yet," he continued, his face getting flushed and his hands tightening into fists. "I am especially upset because my mother, Hera, is siding with this Peace Circle." Smiling then, he glanced toward Eris, his daughter, thinking that no one could tell she represented strife and fear; slim, tall, and elegant as she was, nothing gave her away. Her rough edges hid in her long, dark-painted fingernails and blood-red lips. He watched her take a seat at the table and continued, "It is obvious they are trying to ignore me, and I will not have it."

"Glad to offer all my support, Father," she answered to the slam of his fist against the tabletop. "We will stop them."

Ares came closer and took her hands in his, his smile

reaching his eyes. Eris was the first to offer her support, as the other two were still standing, dusting off their clothes from the journey, listening.

Turning to face them, the god of war finally asked, "What do you say, my sons?"

Phobos, shaking his leonine mane, answered, "Do not fret, dear Father. Zeus is the king of all the gods and claims that he wants to let mortals settle their own battles. If he does not interfere, that gives us lots of room to take people to the battlefields of Athens, Troy, and all around the Mediterranean."

"Come sit by me," Ares said, motioning to his son, who settled next to him, and patting him on his back. Then he turned to Deimos, god of violence, who had come last. He wore full armor and was still standing, gripping his sword by his side. "You aptly serve me," he praised the boy, "raising feelings of dread and terror in warriors before a battle. I am counting on you."

In a whirlwind of excitement, Deimos removed his sword from the sheath, brandishing it in the air. "Hail Ares! I will taunt them with their worst instincts, so that revenge prevails, Father. The gods don't hand their loyalties easily to any cause."

"Go, visit the two kings," Ares said, smiling. "Keep fueling their differences. Be crafty, remind them of their cause, make them proud defenders of their people, and all should work out!" It had worked so many times before that he was certain peace would never come.

TWENTY-FIVE

AN AUSPICIOUS DAY

*T*wo days before the assembly, Helios ensured that the temperatures were kept moderate to make it comfortable for his people as they prepared the new center for the arrival of guests. Every person in the palace worked to wash, shine, and polish the marble bleachers, sweep the terraces, and tie blue and white ribbons with peace messages Clymene had written on the silvery olive trees.

In the early hours of the following morning, Daedalus and Leon tested the irrigation system for the last time. Perse, consumed by her desire for perfection, made frequent visits to the site all day, overseeing the preparations and ordering people around. Her keen eye did not miss even the smallest flaw, as she pointed out a small dirt pile that remained in the center of the orchestra. "Shame," she scolded Leonora, who was running around frantically, trying to meet her mistress's demands.

That night, Perse retired to her bedroom, her body and mind feeling a mix of exhaustion, anxiety, and pride in the accomplishments of the palace staff throughout the day. She sank into her bath in lukewarm water, contemplating the uncertainty of how many guests would attend and despising her own helplessness in the matter. No one could make them come. The lessons of history loomed in her mind, reminding her of the futility of battles and the countless lives lost. The bards had tirelessly recounted the horrors of the ten-year Trojan campaign, yet wars persisted. Millennia of conflict had been on her mind, reminding her that war was worse than useless. In recent years, she had seen so much bloodshed, so many deaths. Poets and scribes had carried the dreadful outcomes of the Trojan War to the people. And yet wars had not stopped. Helios had shared with her Zeus's perspective, that death had been a convenient way to eliminate undesirable mortals and gods alike. After all, the father of all had himself waged battles and slayed Titans with his thunderbolts and had so far shown no interest in the peace movement.

Although she had tried to distract herself, the queen could not keep her mind from recounting the losses that surrounded her in recent years. In her own close family, she had witnessed Phaethon's short life sizzle away because of Zeus's impulsive action. Then his friend Orion and other palace guards had joined Minos's army, and some would never come home; they were the most recent casualties. The limbo of Endymion's life, a plot she had assisted in, truly confused her; that was harder to make sense of. She chalked it up to a case of gods' whimsy— their narrow-minded opinions and capricious nature when it came to humans. Lately, she had been beyond frustrated with Minos's and Aegeus's steadfast refusal to meet and agree to a truce. *Could this be a war that would test the impact of this Peace Circle?*

As the auspicious day approached, the queen was up early to meet the rosy dawn. She carefully selected her attire, choosing her light green tunic that she believed would be best suited for the day, and Leonora agreed that it provided a lovely contrast to her gold jewelry. Her servant had brought out several pieces of jewelry Helios had gifted her, and she chose the earrings with the sunburst and a belt she rarely wore, its buckle depicting Helios riding his chariot. Drawing inspiration from Hera, Perse asked to have her hair styled half up in double-up braids, and she wore the beaded necklace made of precious stones interspersed with lustrous amber knobs. Then she rehearsed her speech, which had earlier met with Helios's and Clymene's approval.

Clymene, the designated greeter of prominent guests, eagerly embraced her role and looked forward to escorting them to their seats, reserved on the front and central rows of the bleachers. Today it delighted her to live in Helios's palace and be an integral part of the peace initiative. She hoped that the agenda they had built would bear results and inspire guests to take action, rather than offer only passive support of the goal. As she prepared for her duties, she took care to create a perfect coiffure. She carefully arranged her curls to flow down her forehead, springing out of her crimson scarf. In a maroon gown, she wore the sun-god's earrings and several golden bracelets that adorned her wrists and jingled with every movement of her hands. Clymene came to fulfill her duties, parting from the drab colors of mourning, making a significant shift in her attire. When she climbed the grand staircase to what they had come to call "the center," she ran into the master architect.

With a sweeping gesture toward the crowd, Daedalus said brightly, "Many have already arrived. It is an unusual honor to be present on such an auspicious occasion!"

"Perse has orchestrated a wonderful event," Clymene said, surveying the vibrant scene before her, a teeming crowd for a mission she wholeheartedly endorsed.

A team of jugglers delighted the crowd, deftly tossing balls and rings into the air, while acrobats showcased their agility, performing backflips and handstands up on the stage. Every now and then, a pair of salpinges would pierce the morning air, signaling the arrival of a distinguished guest. Just at that moment, a prolonged and resonant fanfare announced the arrival of a truly special guest. In the late morning, those present turned to welcome Mother Cybele, with some in the audience clapping and others bowing with awe. The venerable crone, wearing a long, flowing burgundy chiton and her royal turret-crown, arrived in her lion-drawn carriage. It was an enormous honor for Helios's house, for Mother Cybele rarely made appearances. Perse hurried forward and bowed as she kissed her hand, while Helios followed his wife, assisting the revered deity as she gracefully descended from her carriage.

"Mother of all, guardian of nature, gods, mortals, and of warriors in battle, we welcome you to the Circle of Peace," said Clymene, and she led her to her seat.

As Cybele followed Clymene, she gazed around the crowded center and, breaking her silence, declared, "I am thrilled to join you in this delightful setting. Beautiful!" Her presence emanated a serene aura, and she affirmed, "I am here to lend my support to your worthy cause."

Smiling with delight as soon as they saw her, Hera and Artemis, who had just arrived, exchanged kisses on both cheeks and engaged in a friendly conversation. Clymene bowed and left them. Traversing among guests, she maintained a polite smile and attentive ear. She was concerned that alliances and commitments among their guests would fizzle once the day was over. She watched Helios, who in moments like this shone with his gracious and generous countenance, persuading new arrivals to take their seats.

Clymene and her sister approached the regal figure of Hera, inviting her to join them at the center of the amphitheater. The reverent and excited crowd, who had heard rumors, gathered around them anticipating the presentation of the meticulously woven veil Clymene carried. She was clutching the silk veil in her hands, its delicate folds of saffron shimmering in the sunlight. Clymene approached Hera and extended the gift with utmost reverence to the Olympian goddess, who stood tall, emanating an aura of power—yet there was a gentle warmth in her gaze.

Perse stepped forward with measured steps and addressed her, speaking humbly, "Great Hera, we—Clymene and I—have labored tirelessly to create this veil as an offering to your divine presence. Each thread, dyed with care, represents our gratitude for your support, blessings, and guidance." She lowered her gaze for a moment and then continued, her voice steady but filled with emotion. "My sister and I offer this veil to you to serve as a symbol of our eternal devotion, O queen of the gods. May you continue to bless our efforts and help us grow our Peace Circle with all those you favor and protect."

As Perse finished speaking, a hush fell over the crowd, all eyes fixed on Hera, awaiting her response. The goddess regarded the veil with appreciation and grace, and accepting it, wrapped it around her body. "Your devotion pleases me. This veil will forever stand as a testament to the bond we share and our dedication to the mission for peace. I accept the gift with gratitude and offer you my lasting protection and commitment to the cause you have so passionately spearheaded." Hera's gaze swept across the crowd, then returned to Perse. "Now it is your turn to address us," she continued, her voice firm yet inviting. "Speak to us of our purpose that unites us so that we can commit to peace at this remarkable center that Daedalus crafted." The crowd erupted into cheers and applause as Daedalus took a bow. It was a moment that held the promise of unity, forging a path to a common goal.

When the applause died down, Perse stepped forward to address the crowd. Her heart raced with excitement and nerves, and she knew this was her moment. She took a deep breath and began to speak, her voice clear and strong, carrying to every corner of the amphitheater.

"Distinguished guests, honorable Olympians, I stand before you today with immense gratitude and a keen sense of purpose. We have gathered in this magnificent center, crafted by the genius of Master Daedalus, to embark on a mission never undertaken before—a mission that holds the power to transform the world."

The crowd leaned forward to listen as Perse continued, her voice resonating with determination.

"Today we pledge ourselves to the Circle of Peace—a sacred commitment that will foster harmony, understanding, and unity among all beings. In a world often marked by strife and discord, we have chosen to come together and work toward a future where conflicts are resolved through dialogue and compassion."

She paused for a moment, allowing her words to sink in. Looking up, her eyes followed a pair of doves that were flying over the crowd. She smiled.

"People like tidy stories, with a beginning, middle, and end. Wars start, crest, and end with a victor and many deaths. Our mission here is much more complex than that. We defy ends; we seek continuous efforts, one at a time. The human experience is often one of struggle and hardship, where mortals and immortals alike find themselves caught in the tumultuous waves of life. Disagreements, misunderstandings, and conflicts can easily escalate.

"I will recite from Homer for all to hear, for he is the bard who studied the horrific war in Troy and told us about it with unsentimental realism. His vivid descriptions remind us of the mayhem and barbarity that prevailed. He laces his rhapsodies with many graphic descriptions—I think because the wise bard wants to confront us with its brutality. I will recite a brief piece of his. This is the moment Patroclus is slaying Thestor outside Troy: 'Next he sprang on Thestor, son of Enops, who was sitting all huddled up in his chariot, for he had lost his wits and the reins had been torn out of his hands. Patroclus went up to him and drove a spear into his right jaw; he thus hooked him by the teeth and the spear pulled him over the rim of his car, as one who sits at the end of some jutting rock and draws a strong fish out of the sea with a hook and a line—even so with his spear did he pull Thestor all gaping from his chariot. He then threw him down on his face and he died while falling.'"

There was silence in the crowd. A mild breeze flowed through as the pair of doves circled the sky. Perse continued: "We gather not to glorify the horrors of war but to confront it. The image of Patroclus slaying Thestor is a haunting one, a stark reminder of the brutality that can unfold when conflicts escalate beyond control. I shudder when I imagine his death. Peace has a certain magic that we cannot easily describe or quantify. It is a transformative force that has the power to heal wounds, repair relationships, and create a sense of unity and purpose, an alliance between gods and mortals. We must tap into this magic, for it is within our grasp, the key to unlocking the potential for a more peaceful and just world."

Her eyes scanned the crowd, searching for connection and understanding. Perse continued, her words resonating with passion:

"We can dream of the day when a special circle is unnecessary. And to those who did not come because they disagree with our hope that we can intervene and bring peace, I say, 'You can try to ignore us, you can try to dismiss us, you can try to boycott our efforts, but you will never silence our voices for peace.' Together, we can weave a new narrative—one that celebrates unity, understanding, and compassion. This is our mission, and together we can make it a reality! On this joyous occasion, please come and share your thoughts. The day is ours to join together and plan."

Perse stepped away from the podium, tingling with the intensity of her passion. As the crowd roared their support, she was satisfied they had heard her message. Helios's daughters Lampetia and Phaethusa hurried over to her. The three women embraced, and the sisters congratulated Perse for her moving speech. Others followed her with endorsements, their own messages, assurances, and no challenges. She listened and applauded and encouraged more gods to step up and give their vows of support.

Several speakers delivered their ideas, among them Hera and Artemis, and made promises to help. When Eirene, the radiant daughter of Zeus and Themis, took a turn at the podium, she captivated the crowd with the passion and enthusiasm in her voice. She spoke about promoting understanding, choosing and supporting leaders who invest in better communication and their ability to negotiate, their care for the people and desire to maintain prosperity and order in their communities. Eirene's powerful words reminded everyone of the transformative power of peace and the possibilities that lie within reach when gods and mortals come together as one. Her zealous enthusiasm for striving for peace drew applause, but the day was getting long for everyone.

As the speeches continued, Perse's restless mind was already thinking of the opposition. She knew that absent Ares and his allies were likely plotting to disrupt the peace movement. They were working to ensure the conflict and bloodshed continued outside Athens and were looking for opportunities to start other disputes and battles.

TWENTY-SIX

STRENGTH IN UNITY: OVERCOMING OPPOSITION

The festivities were unfolding at the Peace Center, and Ares, the god of war, was notably absent, along with his loyal allies. Fully aware of the momentous event taking place, he had listened intently to his children discussing the significance and potential power of the Peace Circle. Their words ignited a flicker of concern about their morale, and he decided that his people needed a reminder about their joined mission. He called a meeting at the usual tent outside of Troy.

His twin sons were returning from a ceremony outside Athens where Minos's men had slaughtered a bull over a captured shield and painted their hands in the bull's gore. Their presence contributed to an atmosphere charged with eerie intensity. The soldiers had sworn an oath to Ares, Deimos, and Phobos, who delighted in the sight of blood, that either they would level the city and sack the Athenians by force, or in death they would smear the soil with their own blood.

Fearsome Ares rode his smooth-wheeled chariot and dismounted in his shining armor, following the twins, Phobos and Deimos, and found Eris waiting for them in the tent. Inside, the air crackled with anticipation, mirroring the turbulent energy that surrounded the god of war and his chosen allies.

The three sat around the table chatting while Ares rested his shield on the ground and paced around them, keeping his hands knitted together behind his back. When he finally stopped by a chair, he said, "The reason I brought you here today is to remind you that you are strong and capable of taking on any challenge. Together, we are a powerful force. We can beat the Circle of Peace. Now let us show them what we are made of!"

He noticed an enigmatic smile playing on Eris's lips when she pulled out a golden apple from her satchel and raised it, declaring, "A gift from the gods! Today it symbolizes our power and unity of purpose." She offered it to her father, who passed it around, and each one took a piece. He saw that they felt their strength surging through them. Ares motioned for them to stand, and they mirrored him.

"We are a team!" Ares declared, his voice resolute and commanding. "Perse's coalition is just another challenge—one we shall face head-on. Who knows how long it will last? Just remember what we have here today and carry it with you, no matter what comes your way."

Eris chimed in, raising her arm. "We are with you. I will support you, sowing strife and discord in the world."

The god of war nodded in her direction, pleased with her unwavering support, and looked at the other two. "We must stay vigilant, my sons. We must never let them forget the power of our family. Our weapon is the strength we hold in our unity. With that, we can achieve anything." He looked around the table, feeling satisfied. "We will stay unstoppable!"

Glancing at Phobos, Ares saw downcast eyes and sensed his son's concern, so he added, "They think they can create opposition. Soon they will realize that all the altruism in the world does not serve them when they encounter us."

The god of war considered his son again and listened attentively as Phobos voiced his thoughts. "That is a mighty gathering, Father," he began, his tone cautious. "It will take more than sheer force to overcome their ideals and unity."

Eris burst in, interrupting him. "No need to panic, brother. Our weapons and ability to persuade are difficult to counter."

"My power is to build and spread dread," said Deimos.

"And fear," added Phobos unconvincingly, his own power diminished by his waning resolve.

Ares stared at his shield, then moved closer to Phobos, concerned about his son. Patting him on the back, he said, "Remember, Phobos, that Zeus is not supporting them." His words aimed at bolstering his son's spirits, and he continued looking at the others. "In the future, we may have to give in occasionally; perhaps wars will be less frequent. The Circle will work on their mission passionately and may have some success."

His children looked at him, surprised, but as he finished, a sardonic smile spread on his angular face and his voice tinged with irony, ". . . and if you believe in that, you can believe in anything!"

Loud laughter broke out and Ares raised his fist. "Come on, everybody! You have work to do. Sharpen your weapons!" And he walked out of the tent into a day breaking out in pregnant clouds and thunderclaps.

All afternoon, Clymene mingled with visitors, greeting her niece Circe, as well as her Oceanid sisters who had come and other deities whom she was meeting for the first time. Mostly she politely listened to their conversations. But her heart sank as she overheard some whispered discussions. Worse yet, Daedalus confirmed her suspicions. He pointed discreetly toward Hermes and told her, "I overheard Hermes tell his girlfriend, sniggering, 'A lot of megalomaniacs live in Helios's house. They think wars can be stopped! Preposterous!' and rolled his eyes."

It was a revelation to Clymene that not everyone present supported the Circle of Peace. Her curiosity piqued, next she approached a small group that included her sister Oceanids, and Chaos and Erebus. Right away she sensed something amiss. Then she had heard Chaos say, "I support Minos; he will win this war." She noticed their startled reaction and polite yet distant demeanor when she drew near, and she wondered, *What have they been discussing? Are they also against the cause of peace?* She knew from experiences in Ethiopia that alliances, especially in early stages, could easily fizzle, and she knew the journey toward peace could be met with resistance. She remained observant, her interactions filled with a mixture of warmth and caution.

Unexpectedly she ran into the pair of the Aloadae giants, youthful hunters wearing caps and carrying their hunting spears. Their presence surprised her, considering their past involvement in wars. Rumor had it that they had joined the giants who waged war on gods and had defeated Ares in the past. She couldn't help but eavesdrop on their conversation. Perhaps they'd had a change of heart—but then she heard one say, "Zeus is not behind the peace movement, and Ares respects us; he would welcome us back as allies. Time to leave this gathering, brother. We don't belong. But the site is amazing. Worth a stop." She watched them move away, looking for a way out.

Feeling a sense of urgency, Clymene knew she had to take action. She made her way to the podium. Her intention was clear—to draw attention, to rally support, and to counteract the negative influence of those who opposed the Circle of Peace.

As she approached the podium, her presence commanded the attention of those around her. She stood tall, radiating determination and resolve. The conversations around her dwindled as all eyes turned toward Clymene.

Her voice rang out, "Dear fellow members of the Peace Circle, my name is Clymene, and I greet you as a member of the House of Helios and Perse's sister. We have heard inspiring talks from many. I believe you know the cause of peace is worthy. So, I urge you, let this not be all buildup that leads nowhere. In my mind's eye, I see fields streaming young men's blood, bodies lying moveless, shadows crowding in Hades, and I know our dear ones demand more. Many have shed tears for losing loved ones, but tears are not enough. We owe more to those departed and to ourselves.

"Leaders and warriors must come to the table, realizing that their actions led to bloody fields, loss of life, and grieving families. They owe sacrifices to the gods and goddesses to give them wisdom and guidance. You who support peace, help them find ways to create truces and end the bloodshed in peace. They owe the world self-awareness that leads to tucking away their egos, false pride, and bravado to seek ways to reconcile."

Her words hung in the air, underscoring the importance of self-awareness and humility. Clymene continued, her voice filled with determination.

"We face a current challenge: the bloody battle outside Athens. I won't leave this meeting before we have envoys to draw the kings of Athens and Crete to the table. Step forward if you are ready to take part in this mission."

She had spoken the truth. Helios and Perse began to applaud, and slowly the crowd joined them as the pair stepped onto the stage, next to Clymene, who called out again with a stentorian voice: "Let those ready to commit to action step forward!"

Zeus reclined on his throne on top of Mount Olympus, sipping his ambrosia, and although he looked calm and indifferent, he was well tuned in to the proceedings of the newborn Circle of Peace. This afternoon, all the other Olympians were away except for his favorite daughter, Athena. He spotted several familiar faces at Helios's palace—his oppositional wife, Hera, among them—and was amazed at the number attending the event.

He broke the silence, voicing his surprise, "So many have gone to this gathering! They seem passionate about the cause; some may be subversive."

Athena looked at him with a wily smile. "Or merely curious, Father."

Zeus saw that she was ready to say more. "Shush! I want to watch and hear their speeches. I realize this is a conspicuous cause and it is an auspicious meeting, daughter."

She moved away and took a seat quietly. He kept his silence, but when he heard Clymene and Helios issue their final challenges to the crowd, he was deeply moved. His eyes gleamed and he stood up, watching the amphitheater and counting aloud those moving to the front. ". . . twelve, thirteen . . . They are young, both men and women; several of my children are among them." He stopped and added, uncharacteristically giddy, "I count fourteen! There are more still moving to the front!"

He knew Athena to be fair-minded, but he saw that she rolled her eyes and he heard the hint of exasperation when she said, "You know, Ares is plotting how to thwart any efforts as you speak. They need a god who champions peace, Father, if they would stand a chance."

Zeus, thoughtful, took a deep breath. She was right. There ought to be a goddess who would champion this cause. "You are right! I will give peace a chance," he declared, his gaze shifting toward the volunteers, looking for the ideal candidate to carry out this mission. "And who better to appoint than a daughter of mine to champion peace." It had been a long time since he had appointed anyone to new responsibilities.

Ever wise, Athena offered, "Consider Eirene. She stepped forward and spoke well at the Circle of Peace assembly." After a moment, she added, "Her mother, Themis, your bride, has been your counselor and guided you wisely in matters of divine law, and her daughter has always leaned into peacemaking; besides, that is what her name means!"

He saw the merit of Athena's advice. "Yes, she stepped forward to help, and her name already means peace." Sitting back down on his throne, he ordered his daughter, "Ask her mother to bring her over once they disperse. Besides, mortals need to have hope. I loved Perse's challenge, and her words are powerful." In his mind, the father of all replayed Perse's words: *We can dream of the day when a special circle is unnecessary. And to those who did not come because they disagree with our hope that we can intervene and bring peace, I say, "You can try to ignore us, you can try to dismiss us, you can try to boycott our efforts, but you will never silence our voices for peace."*

Zeus was fully persuaded. "Clymene's call to action came at the right moment. They deserve a champion. This will be Perse's legacy to the world!"

It was a turning point. The flame of hope for peace was here to stay.

GLOSSARY

GODS

AEETES: Son of Helios and Perse, Circe's brother. He is a sorcerer who reigns in the Kingdom of Colchis. His name comes from the ancient Greek word that means "eagle."

AEOLUS: The god of winds, he appears in Homer's *Odyssey* giving Odysseus a bag containing storm winds to protect him from danger. Unfortunately, greedy companions open the bag looking for gold, and the winds lead the ship back to Aeolus's island.

ALOADAE GIANTS: Two giants who attempt to storm the home of the gods by piling three mountains—Olympus, Ossa, and Pelion—one on top of the other, defeating Ares, who tries to stop them.

APOLLO: Son of Zeus and Leto, Apollo is one of the twelve gods of Mount Olympus. He is the god of music, poetry, light, prophecy, and medicine. He was born and worshipped on the island of Delos, where mortals built him a magnificent temple.

ARES: Greek god of war, he is the son of Zeus and Hera, and one of the twelve Olympians.

ATHENA: One of the twelve gods of Mount Olympus, daughter of Zeus, and the goddess of battle strategy and wisdom. She is also the goddess of victory. She is always accompanied by her owl. Odysseus is a mortal under her protection.

CHAOS: She was the first of the primordial gods (Protogenoi) to emerge at the dawn of creation.

CIRCE: Ancient Greek goddess, an enchantress, and a minor goddess in Greek mythology. She is the daughter of the god Helios and the Oceanid nymph Perse. Circe is renowned for her vast knowledge of potions and herbs. In Homer's *Odyssey*, she changes a band of Odysseus's men into pigs, takes Odysseus as a lover, and eventually aids them as they depart for their home in Ithaca.

CLYMENE: An Oceanid nymph, wife to King Merops of Ethiopia, and mother of Phaethon, a son from an illicit affair with Helios. In Greek mythology, the name *Clymene* or Κλυμένη means "fame."

CYBELE: Great mother of gods, predominant in Greek literature. She is the mistress of wild nature (symbolized by her constant companion, the lion), a healer, the goddess of fertility, and protectress in time of war.

DEIMOS and PHOBOS: Twin gods or personified spirits (daimones) of fear. Deimos represents terror and dread; Phobos embodies panic, flight, and rout. They are sons of the war-god Ares and accompany their father into battle, driving his chariot and spreading fear in his wake. Sons of Aphrodite, goddess of love, the twins also represent fear of loss.

DEMETER: The Olympian goddess of harvest and agriculture, presiding over grains and the fertility of the earth. When Hades, the brother of Zeus and god of the underworld, abducts her daughter, Persephone, Demeter goes in search of her child. When she cannot find her, she refuses to let anything grow.

The final compromise is to release her daughter to her mother for half the year and keep her in Hades the other half. When Demeter has her daughter, nature flourishes in spring and summer, giving crops and brightness to people.

EIRENE: The goddess and personification of peace, daughter of Themis and Zeus. She is depicted in art as a beautiful young woman carrying a cornucopia, scepter, and torch.

EREBUS: The god of a dark region of the underworld and the personification of darkness.

HECATE: The chief goddess presiding over magic and spells. She witnesses the abduction of Persephone, Demeter's daughter, to the underworld and, torch in hand, assists in the search for her.

HELIOS: Helios (also Hellios) is the god of the sun in Greek mythology. He rides a golden chariot that brings the sun across the sky each day from the east to the west. He is married to Perse and is Circe and Aeetes's father.

HEPHAESTUS: The crippled son of Zeus and Hera, famous for his skills for smithing weapons for the gods and protector of blacksmiths, sculptors, and fire.

HERA: The queen of gods and wife/sister of Zeus, she is the goddess of marriage and protector of women during and after childbirth.

HERMES: Son of Zeus, he is the herald of the gods and protector of human heralds, travelers, thieves, merchants, and orators. He moves freely between the worlds of the mortal and the divine, aided by his winged sandals.

HESTIA: The Olympian virgin goddess of hearth and home. She is the firstborn daughter of the mighty Titan Cronus and is often quoted as saying, "Sometimes the hardest power to master is the power of yielding."

IRIS: The goddess of the rainbow that links heaven and earth, and Hera's messenger.

LAMPETIA: Daughter of Helios and Neaera. Her name means "shining." She and her twin sister, Phaethusa, guard the cattle and sheep of Trinacia.

MINOS: King of Crete and son of Zeus and Europa. He has Daedalus build the labyrinth in which the Minotaur is kept. The Minoan civilization is named after the mythical king. The best-known Minoan ruin is the Palace of Knossos, which is so full of nooks and crannies that it resembles a labyrinth.

MOIRAI: Three goddesses (the Fates) of ancient Greece who together personify fate: Clotho, the spinner of life; Lachesis, who measures the length of life; and Atropos, who cuts the thread of each life.

PACIFAE: An Oceanid nymph, known for her witchcraft. She is the daughter of Helios and Perse, and the queen of Crete, married to Minos.

PERSE: In Greek mythology, Perse is an Oceanid nymph and one of Helios's wives. She is the mother of Circe, Aeetes, Pacifae, and other lesser-known children.

PHAETHON: His name means "the shining." He is the son of Helios by the Oceanid Clymene, the wife of Merops, king of Ethiopia.

PHAETHUSA: In Greek mythology, Phaethusa is a daughter of Helios and Neaera. She is the personification of the brilliant, blinding rays of the sun. She and her twin sister, Lampetia, guard the cattle and sheep of Trinacia.

PHOBOS and DEIMOS: See DEIMOS and PHOBOS.

POSEIDON: One of the twelve gods of Olympus, the god of the sea (and of water generally), earthquakes, dolphins, and horses.

RIVER STYX: The principal river that separates the world of the living from Hades, circling the underworld seven times, thus separating it from the land of the living.

SELENE: The goddess and personification of the moon. She is traditionally identified as the daughter of the Titans Hyperion and Theia, and sister of the sun-god Helios and the dawn goddess Eos.

TETHYS: One of the Titans, offspring of Uranus (Sky) and Gaia (Earth). She married Oceanus, an enormous river encircling the world, and by him is the mother of numerous sons (river gods) and numerous daughters (the Oceanids), among them Perse and Clymene.

THEMIS: The goddess and personification of justice, divine order, law, and custom. She is one of the twelve Titan children of Gaia and Uranus, and the second wife of Zeus. She is often depicted holding scales.

XENIOS ZEUS: Zeus is sometimes called "Xenios Zeus" in his role as a protector of strangers. He thus embodies the moral obligation to be hospitable to foreigners and guests.

ZEUS: The sky and thunder god in ancient Greek religion. He rules as king of the gods of Mount Olympus. His symbols are the thunderbolt, eagles, bulls, and oak trees.

MORTALS AND MORE

AEAEA: A mythological island said to be the home of the goddess-sorceress Circe, on the Aegean Sea.

ATHENS: An ancient Greek city-state, considered the birthplace of democracy and the idea that all citizens should have a voice in governing their society.

CHITON: A long woolen tunic worn in Ancient Greece.

CRETE: The largest Greek island. The most famous mythical king of Crete is Minos, for whom Daedalus built the labyrinth to house the Minotaur.

DAEDALUS: Famous engineer, architect, and inventor. He built the labyrinth to house the Minotaur for Minos, king of Crete. To escape from Crete, he builds wings made from feathers and wax for himself and his son, Icarus, who plunges into the sea and drowns.

ENDYMION: A beautiful youth, a shepherd, and Selene's lover, placed in eternal sleep.

HIMATION: An outer garment worn by the ancient Greeks over the left shoulder and under the right.

HOMER: Greek poet who is credited as the author of the *Iliad* and the *Odyssey*, two epic poems that are foundational works of ancient Greek literature. Homer is considered one of the most revered and influential authors in history.

ICARUS: Son of Daedalus, he receives wings constructed of feathers and wax from his father so they can flee Crete. While crossing the sea, Icarus ignores his father's warnings and flies too close to the sun. The wax melts, and he falls into the water and drowns.

LEKYTHOS: An oil flask used at baths and gymnasiums and for funerary offerings, characterized by a long cylindrical body gracefully tapered to the base and a narrow neck with a loop-shaped handle.

LEONORA: Perse's trusted head servant who manages the palace staff and carries out her mistress's orders. The character was created by the author to play her part in this novella.

MELPOMENE: Clymene's trusted servant who serves her in Helios's palace. The character was created by the author to play her part in this novella.

MEROPS: King of Ethiopia, husband of Clymene, and adoptive father of Phaethon, his wife's son by Helios.

MESSINA: The Strait of Messina is said to be where the sea monster Skylla and Charybdis waited for ships and sailors to devour.

METOPE: Square terra-cotta frieze plaques, often bearing mythological scenes.

ODYSSEUS: A legendary character, king of the island of Ithaca who fought in the Trojan War. He is known for his intellect and cunning. Homer tells of his adventures of returning home after the end of the Trojan War in the *Odyssey*. He lives on Circe's island for a year before departing for his home in Ithaca.

ORION: A young man and friend of Phaethon. The character was created by the author to play his part in this novella.

PAEAN: A song of praise or triumph.

PEPLOS: A rich outer robe or shawl worn by women in ancient Greece, hanging in loose folds and sometimes drawn over the head.

SKYLLA: A sea-monster who haunts the rocks of a narrow strait opposite the whirlpool of Charybdis. Ships that sail too close to her rocks in the Strait of Messina, between Sicily and Italy, lose sailors to her ravenous, darting heads.

THESPIAN: An actor. The word is related to Thespis, the man who first took the stage in ancient Greece. As an adjective, the word *thespian* describes someone who is related to drama.

TROY: City at the entrance to the Hellespont and the center of Priam's kingdom. Homer's *Iliad* and the *Odyssey* are epics about the Trojan War. Troy is destroyed at the end of the ten-year war.

Read on for a special preview
of the debut book of the 'Greek Tale' series

AN UNEXPECTED ALLY:

A GREEK TALE OF LOVE, REVENGE, AND REDEMPTION

BY SOPHIA KOUIDOU—GILES

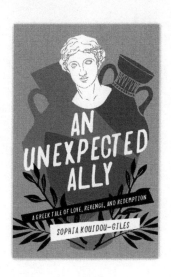

"*H*ow do we know the ones we love? Do we? Do we really love them, or are they companions for a time?" Circe was in one of her moods. She was working on another tapestry, chatting with her faithful servant, Melis.

"Mistress," Melis offered, wringing her hands. "All you have to do is choose your man. Who can resist you? Who has ever resisted you before?"

The all-knowing enchantress smiled to herself, for she saw her servant was trying to lift her out of her melancholy. Pointing to the tangled-up spools and threads stacked by the wall, she ordered, "Sort by color." Melis rolled up her sleeves and followed instructions.

For an instant, immortal Circe believed Melis's words. She could conquer him, this creature she had recently seen in her dreams. He might be a good prospect to follow Odysseus, a man who was no longer in love with her but who had stolen her heart. There had been times she thought of keeping him, slipping him a potion, forcing him to stay, but then she would kill what she loved about him, his moxie, his willpower, his independence. She did not want to keep him tamed, a creature bent to her will.

Melis fastened her black bandana around her graying hair and bent down to collect what had fallen on the floor. "Odysseus is homesick," she mumbled.

Circe only glanced toward her servant before returning to her own thoughts. Despite her affection for the cunning warrior, the enchantress was almost ready to release him. "He deserves his fate: meandering the seas in search of Ithaca," she declared with a smirk.

Melis's eyes lit up. "Maybe it's time . . . but you will have no trouble finding another." After all, to beguile and allure were part and parcel of Circe's charms; she rarely needed to use her incantations in matters of the heart.

Circe, the daughter of Helios, the mighty Titan, and the ocean nymph Perse, left her loom and picked up her golden mirror. A pair of wide-set blue-green eyes stared back from a young woman's face, the hair parted with a fine bone comb and tossed to the right. Her skin was smooth and supple. Her chin was pointed, the mark of a decisive woman. Her voluptuous lips tempted every man she ever wanted to pair up with. She touched up her hair. *That's better*, she thought, and smiled, satisfied.

The goddess felt Melis's gaze follow her. Circe had confided to her that the newest object of her curiosity was exotic, fascinating, immortal, a creature of the land and the sea. Like her, he had a deep knowledge of herbs and the gift of prophecy; that made him an equal, an intriguing first for a partner. His name was Glaucus. He had been transformed from an everyday fishmonger to an amphibian god, or so she had heard from Odysseus's crew.

When the servant finished tidying up, she excused herself. Alone again, Circe walked over to her collection of threads and fabrics. She chose a couple of skeins of blue thread and took them to the loom, but she was done working for the day. Over the eons, she had tired from so many losses. However, she could not quiet her thoughts. Could this god be who she hoped for, an immortal companion for an immortal sorceress? Immortality was not all it was cracked up to be. She definitely wanted to have a hand in shaping her own fortune. But life could be unpredictable; there were complicated alliances between Olympian gods and humans. Tides often shifted; she had been caught in those eddies herself from time to time.

On her way to the kitchen, in a swirl of confusion, Melis was puzzling about her lady's plight. She knew Circe to be a powerful woman who did not trust people and relied on her own instincts about things. Her mistress was lonely and chose her lovers well—but an amphibian? What would that be like? Odysseus had come, stayed for a year, and would soon be gone. She knew he was the only one ever to abandon her mistress. That must smart.

Melis did not keep Circe's confidences to herself. She stopped to taste some figs the girls had plucked from an overloaded tree, so ripe they were dripping honey, and shared the news. "Circe is interested in an amphibian god. She has been asking questions, gathering every tidbit she can from Odysseus himself and his men," she said, with a smug smile. All ears perked up and soon it was the whisper of the day. "They come and they go . . . They come and they go . . ."

Some had sympathy. "She is upset. Odysseus is leaving her," said the washerwoman, still scrubbing pots and pans.

"Give her time to get over him," added her helper.

Others were in disbelief: "Such a crazy idea." They all wondered if all the witchcraft in the world could make this relationship work. She was of the land, he of the sea.

Then the talk shifted to Circe's past affairs and lovers. Melis reminded them that any human would eventually die and leave her alone once more. The girls liked those who gave them small gifts to thank them for their services. Not everybody did. "Remember the ribbons I got?" said the pretty one.

"I remember, but he liked me better. He gave me a belt made of shells," answered the one watching the cauldron simmering over the coals.

"What would an amphibian give us?" wondered the third. "More sea trinkets?" They giggled and started listing what they would like to receive.

"What matters most is what Circe gives you, girls," said Melis, who had fed the gossip but did not care for their greed and squabbles.

Earlier in the week on a particular evening, Circe's servers had been waiting for her to take her place next to Odysseus at the table and begin dining as they did every night. She was late. As she rushed along the halls, her gauzy tunic fanning out behind her, she had not yet settled on a plan of action. That afternoon, roaming alone in the forest, she had debated whether to grant Odysseus's plea to release him. Her steps had taken her to the uncovered pigsty where his men, still in pig form as they'd been since the day she'd first cast her spell, were guttling the roots and greens her slave girls had poured into the troughs.

Invisible, she rested on a fallen tree trunk behind some tall palm trees and listened to their conversation. "We'll never see Ithaca again," a couple of them mourned, rolling in the mud to cool down from the hot day. After a year in the pigsty, even hardened warriors were giving up hope. Circe knew she held their fortunes.

Elpinikis, one of Odysseus's lead men, spoke up. "Odysseus will convince Circe to let us leave her island and return home to Ithaca." He walked around the pen looking at each sailor in the eye: "Remember the prophecy Glaucus gave us. We *will* get away. Odysseus is crafty and soon we'll board our ship. We have overcome so many obstacles. Glaucus told us we would see our home again."

Circe's ears perked up. It was the first time she heard of Glaucus. Who might that be? She approached the pigsty, staying a few feet away from the muddy ground, and called Elpinikis by his name.

"Who is this Glaucus?"

Surprised, the white swine moved closer to the sorceress, making his voice humble: "What do you want to know, mighty Circe?"

"What did he prophesy?" Her eyes narrowed. "Who and where is he?"

Despite his piggish form, she saw that the young man was reluctant to share much. "He was an everyday fishmonger, my goddess," he tried, laconic as ever. "But now he is immortal: a god, with the divine gift of prophecy. He gave us hope we will return home someday."

"Where did you meet him?" she asked, tilting her head.

"In Delos, when we all swam in the calm waters of that bay."

"Is he really a god?" she persisted, intrigued by the unexpected information.

"That is what Odysseus said. Ask him," Elpinikis answered, moving away and lowering his head to get a drink of water. Circe read his mind, felt his fear, and sensed his yearning to see her notorious magic wand that had transformed kings and slaves alike. She knew he would never beg for what he most wanted: for her to shift them back to their old selves.

Noticing the setting sun, Circe realized she was holding up dinner. She rushed away, following a path inhabited by birds she had transformed from human enemies. They chirped pleasing songs to the enchantress.

Up ahead, she could see that her servers had already set the table for two. She and Odysseus met there every night no matter where their day took them. Odysseus, the king of Ithaca and leader of men, had been repairing the ship, moored on the bay. A short man, dark-skinned and muscular, with small dark eyes and an unkempt beard, he liked working with his rough hands. Circe tracked his progress. By now he had most everything in good shape. She knew he worried about her delaying their departure. To watch him, though, sipping wine diluted with water from the wide-mouthed cylix that the slave girls kept refilling for him, no one would know he was fretting. It was time for the biggest meal of the day, and he would be hungry. Circe moved so silently that no one could hear the pitter-patter of her feet, and she took her seat across from him without an apology. "Have you kept busy today?"

Looking surprised, he swallowed a bite of cheese and reached for a fig. "Busy making some last repairs to the ship. My sailors and I are ready to leave. Another day when home is calling, Circe." The pleading in his eyes forced her to recognize that their affair had to be over soon. She had promised him she would return his men to their human form when the time came.

In a sharp, almost accusing tone, she said, "You have some guidance from Glaucus for your trip back home, I understand. You have never mentioned him. Is he credible?"

She refilled his cylix herself and watched Odysseus take a moment, thoughtful, staring at the image drawn on the bottom of it: Apollo wearing a laurel wreath on his head. She smiled to herself, noticing the king of Ithaca's surprise that she was aware of Glaucus. "Is he a man or an immortal god?" she pressed.

"A god," he answered carefully. "Beautiful and unusual, he shifted in form from human to an amphibian creature, growing fins instead of arms and a fish tail instead of legs. He knows about life's mysteries and has the gift of prophecy."

Circe motioned for Odysseus to go on.

"He certainly knows a lot about herbs. Many go to Delos to ask him about the future."

"What else do you know?" Her eyes stayed on him.

"Nothing more." He shrugged. "Some gods want to see us back home and others don't. He was sympathetic." He took a breath and looked away from her. "But where is our meal?"

She snapped her fingers to signal to the servers that they were ready for more food. They rushed in a platter with fish and asparagus and they filled their plates, eating until Circe complained to the slaves. "Wait until we have come to the table before you steam the fish. It's cold. I can barely eat it." She knew it was her own fault for being late. Still, they were there to serve them perfect meals.

They finished with a handful of ripe, delicious figs Circe had ordered her maids to gather from the garden. Not ready to call it a night, and since the evening was mellow, they moved to the patio where Odysseus told stories about a couple of constellations that he knew well from navigating the seas. Shifting his weight from one foot to the other, he pointed to the Pleiades, the six sisters Zeus had turned to pigeons and sent to the night sky to shine like diamonds and help sailors find their way. Close to them was amorous Orion, son of Poseidon, a hunter in pursuit of the sisters. Odysseus had a charming way with words and Circe enjoyed his illuminating stories, but it was getting late and the couple withdrew to their bedroom.

That night Apollo, the lord of Delos, who was fond of the enchantress, sent Circe a vivid dream. He and the other Olympians watched and interfered in her affairs from time to time. The image was of a man rowing his boat out to sea. The man was tall, with long hair that danced in the breeze. His youthful face glowed under the rays of a full moon. He set his rod to the bottom of his boat, dropped anchor, and baited his fishing hook. Circe's gaze sank under the surface of a sapphire sea, discerning the form of a woman who looked familiar; it was her mother, Perse, the ocean nymph, her braided black hair coming loose as she approached Glaucus's boat. She took the fishing hook dangling in the water and forced a fish to swallow it. Then she stood by to watch what the fishmonger would do. Sensing the pull on his line, the man netted the fish and was about to drop it into his bucket but hesitated. He held it for an instant, as though feeling its life quivering away, then released it back to the salty sea, delivering it back to life. With a look of relief on his face, he dipped his oars into the water and steered his vessel to shore.

The dream jarred Circe awake. She did not wake Odysseus. Her mind was racing. It was rare to see her mother in her dreams. The two women were not close and Perse's relationship with Helios was everything Circe was afraid of, a conflicted, humorless pairing. Her mother must be away from the palace again, after some spat with him—although she never talked about their fights openly. *What was she doing following a fishmonger in the sea? What was she doing showing up in my dream? Who was the creature?* She liked to take her dreams apart, to unravel their messages, but this one was puzzling. *Maybe dreams don't mean a thing.* Her gaze shifted toward the moon, still high in its night sky. There would be hours still until morning. *But maybe,* she thought, forcing her eyes back shut, *they mean everything.*

ACKNOWLEDGMENTS

*T*his novella would not have been possible without the support and encouragement of so many people. I particularly want to thank my author groups for being part of early reviews as well as drafts and redrafts of the English version. Efi Metaxa has been a dedicated beta reader of my draft translations of this book into Greek, and Christine Collenette is an expert website and social media support. Susan Meyers and Jean Gilbertson are amazing editors who were always supportive and accessible.

Much of my preparation for this project came from author groups and classes. I would like to thank my teachers, Brenda Peterson, Theo Nestor, Susan Meyers, Scott Driscoll, and others from the Salish Sea Writers and Hugo House. They helped me improve and stay committed to finishing this project.

I am indebted to She Writes Press, especially to Brooke Warner and Shannon Green who shepherded this book into the world and Christine Collenette, Cristina Deptula, Seattle She Writes Press Writers, and my 2023 Cohort who have done more than I ever could to market, promote, and share ideas and support all along.

Finally, I am grateful to my grandsons who are fond of their Greek heritage and have enjoyed reading stories with Ancient Greek heroes and heroines. That has made my work so much more meaningful.

ABOUT THE AUTHOR

Sophia Kouidou-Giles was born in Thessaloniki, Greece, and university educated in the USA. Her work has appeared in *Voices*; *Persimmon Tree*; *Assay*; *The Raven's Perch*; *Storywits*; *Women Writers, Women's Books*; *The Fantasy Hive*; and *The Blue Nib*. Her poetry chapbook is *Transitions and Passages*. Her work has appeared in anthologies including *The Time Collection*, *Visual Verse*, and *Art in the Time of Unbearable Crisis*. She is also the author of the memoir Επιστροφή Στη Θεσσαλονίκη/*Return to Thessaloniki*, published in Greek (Tyrfi Press); *Sophia's Return: Uncovering My Mother's Past* (She Writes Press); and the novella *An Unexpected Ally* (She Writes Press). Kouidou-Giles loves music, walking outdoors, and travel. She lives in the Pacific Northwest, near her son, daughter-in-law, and two grandsons.

For more information and updates, visit:
https://sophiakouidougiles.com.